RAISE YOUR SHIELD

A Novel

Book 3 Of The HOLD FAST Series

CYNTHIA HARRIS

For my friends at Prestonfield House —

ISBN: 9798367309454

Cover art and design by Jared Frank

Printed in the United States of America

This is dedicated to all the women
who **raise their shields** every day to
protect their hearts and those they love

Trigger Warning:

*This novel deals with some mental health struggles
in the aftermath of sexual assault and miscarriage.
While the author has taken great lengths to ensure
the subject matter is dealt with in a compassionate and
respectful manner, the content may be triggering to some readers.*

CHAPTERS

ONE
What You Can Control

Dunmara Castle
Isle of Skye, Scotland
March 1767

The days and weeks passed slowly after the wedding celebration and our return to Dunmara Castle on Skye. I stopped eating fully but said nothing to anyone who asked. I could be caught sipping broth by the fire to keep my belly warm from the chill. I thought that was enough. At least, I *hoped* that was enough.

I became obsessed with not eating, but I could feel myself becoming thin and weak. The weakness showed most with drink. I was now living on wine and whisky and did not even bother to try to soak either up with my beloved bread and butter. I also never told Missus Gerrard about the wonders of fried ham and tatties for breakfast because I no longer cared about either. There was more at work in my mind, but I could not acknowledge it, because I would feel more shame than I already did.

"Good morning," I said, as I leaned across Will's chest to kiss him.

I sat on top of his hips and kept moving above him as he rose to meet me. His hands on my knees, he whispered, *"Take off yer shift."*

"No," I whispered back with a sly smile.

He moved his hands up my thighs and I winced for a moment. Startled by my reaction, he asked, "Did I hurt ye, lass?"

"No," I said, trying to distract him with a flurry of kisses once again.

"I can tell that I did, and I can feel it myself," he said as he lifted the edge of my shift to reveal a large gash on my leg that had just started healing.

"What is this?"

I slowly tried to pull back away from him while tugging down the sleeves of my shift as I said nothing. I did not fool the man for a second, and he sat up immediately saying, "Give me yer arm."

I looked at him, knowing that revealing my arm was going to hurt us both. I tried to deflect and kissed him again, and said, "I am fine, love! Ye didna hurt me. Why are ye asking this? *I am fine!*"

"Give me yer arm," he ordered me coldly and without emotion. He did not wait for me to comply and forcibly grabbed my hand. I started to pull away from him, but eventually let him take it. Honestly, I do not think I could spend many more nights hiding under my shift with my husband.

He took my left hand and pushed the sleeve up to expose fresh cuts and healing scars on the inside of my forearm and wrist. The wrist he loves most. William kissed it tenderly, as he always had, and I could see the pain in his face when he did so. I felt his tenderness, but I mostly felt the shame of what he had just seen. He knows that I did this to myself.

"My love," he said in heartbreak and confusion. Before I could say anything, he pushed me aside on the bed and yelled, "Where is it? Where is the sgian-dubh?!"

I said nothing, and he yelled even louder to me, "Where is the *goddamned blade!?*"

I could not speak to him for the shock of seeing him so angry to curse at me so. He spoke words and in a tone he has never used with me before. I was hurt, but I turned slowly and reached under my pillow. I obediently handed him the sgian-dubh he gave me to protect me after the attack in Edinburgh. He may never understand how this black knife protected me for so many days since.

"I have watched ye since we returned here to the castle. Ye have not been eating and *now this?* Why, love?"

The shame of it all must have shown on my face. I cannot hide my feelings from him. My face betrays me every time.

"Do ye not think I can tell when ye sit next to me at the head table that ye dinnae eat and just push food from one side of yer plate to the other? Do ye not think that I havena noticed that ye suddenly cannae hold yer drink? Do ye not think that when ye lie with me that I feel just yer bones beneath me?"

I raised my hands to my face as my tears formed to match his. With each question he asked, I felt a new pain in my heart. I could not answer any of his questions as I could not speak at all for the immense shame I felt.

3

"Do ye not think I cannae tell that ye are starting to close yerself off from everyone who loves ye? Why?"

Will saw my reaction and changed his tone and said in a way that I had not expected, softly and gently, *"Christ above! Why are ye hurting yer precious and beautiful body?"*

I could feel my tears burn hot now on my cheeks and bit my bottom lip. I believe Will deserves an answer, but it is not something I have thought about having to explain to another. I am afraid I do not have the words for him to understand what I am trying so desperately to understand myself.

"Because..." I started to say and had to put the thoughts I wanted to bury deep within myself into words for another to possibly understand, *"... because* when I hurt myself, I dinnae think about *anyone else* hurting me."

Will's face broke my heart on these words, and he lowered his head to my chest and cried. Now I was no longer hurting just myself, I was hurting another. I felt the pure shame of it on top of my own pain and cried with him. I shut my eyes and put both of my hands in his curls and said, "I am in control of my *own* feelings... feelings that are constantly out of control. I have felt Calder's ghost haunt me since we left Edinburgh, and I am in a blind panic every day. Sometimes I cannae breathe the fear and dread of him takes me so. And as the next clan chief, being back here at Dunmara, I only feel more pressure upon me. I am so sorry, my love, but I dinnae ken how to stop. *This is the only power I have!"*

William collected himself and sat up to look me in the eye. As I cried before him "That is *not* true! But, love, when did ye last eat a meal? A proper meal! Not sipping broth by the fire."

4

"I had most of my breakfast the day we arrived at Mallaig," I said honestly, with my head bowed in shame and in anticipation of his reaction to such a notion. He wasted no time.

"That was over three weeks ago! We will correct that this night! I will have Missus Gerrard make me a plate, even if I have to feed ye myself!"

"Will, dinnae be *angry*," I asked him softly as the tears kept flowing on his words. I wanted to tell him that his genuine concern, love, and fear for me sounded like anger. But he saw my face and heard my words and immediately tried to calm himself.

"And when did ye start using the blade?" he asked softly now.

"I suppose the same day," I said in a whisper and touching the small red scar on my left hand. "It was by accident at first. Remember? I cut my hand with my knife when I was pretending to eat at the tavern and Duncan made his joke?"

"Aye, I remember."

"Once we arrived here at the castle, I remembered how the pain of the cut felt good to me," I said, mesmerized by the memory, and still rubbing the small scar on my hand. "I watched the blood and thought about what a release it was. It was some comfort to me and a reminder that... that I was alive and not dead."

"Och, my darlin' lass," Will said, putting his chin down to his chest again.

"At first, I felt some power and comfort that it was there—even just in my skirt. I liked knowing it was there and spun it around. Then I ran the blade over the skin. But light touches with the blade became scratches. And then scratches became cuts. I tried it in a place I thought I could hide... at least for a while. But when I cut my thigh," I said, touching the painful wound underneath my shift, "I began to worry that I was making deeper wounds and that I couldna keep it from ye fer long."

He looked at me with tears in his eyes. I knew that he was hurting for me that he, even as my husband and protector, could not save me from myself.

I started to shake and said honestly through my tears, "I am *scared* that the wounds are getting bigger and deeper, *to dull a pain that only seems to grow.*"

"I appreciate ye telling me the truth of it, my love, I do! Stay here and I will find the healer. I dinnae ken his name, but I want him to look at yer cuts to ensure they heal properly."

I just whispered, rubbing the scars on my arm for strength, *"Master Morrison."*

"Aye, stay here! Morrison and I will return in a moment to help ye."

He left me and I pulled my knees to my chest and cried because what I thought was my own torment, no longer was. I know that I have now hurt my husband as much as I hurt myself.

+++

Will picked me up off of the floor in front of the fire and placed me upon the bed. I was only half-awake. I could hear him tell the healer what had happened before, but he said, looking at my bloodstained shift, "She has done it again!"

"Not to worry," Master Morrison said calmly as he joined me on the side of my bed.

"What in the devil is this?" I heard Duncan say as he came into the room behind them.

I looked through my tears into the eyes of the healer as he slowly described to me what he was doing as he lifted my shift just high enough to show the wound on my thigh. He said softly that he would help me with the other scars and cuts on my arm.

"Where is the blade, Alex? *Where is it!?*" William yelled to me, looking all around the floor in front of the fire, where he found me.

Duncan said, looking around the hearth and under the chairs with him, "I see no blade on the floor, man."

"I took her sgian-dubh this night," he said, pulling the blade in its sheath from the back of his breeches and showing it to Duncan, "there must be another blade hidden here fer her to have done this again!"

Master Morrison spoke up calmly and said as he held up my right hand for them to see, "No sir, look here! The lady used her own fingernails to open the recent wound on her thigh. It was barely healed, so it was easy to do."

William and Duncan came around the bed to see the jagged nails on my hand covered in blood.

"Och Christ," Duncan said as William knelt beside me, heartbroken that I would do such a thing to myself. I could tell the man was holding and kissing my bloodied hand, but I could not speak.

"Lady MacLeod, drink this fer me please," Morrison said, lifting my head up slightly so I could drink his broth. I was fading from the loss of blood and my own shame but heard him say, "It looks worse than it is, sir. I think she just fainted before the fire, but I have given her a draft of valerian root and chamomile in warm broth. She will calm herself and perhaps sleep fer a few hours."

"She needs to," Duncan said, sternly and in judgement of what he has witnessed. I tried to tell them both that I was sorry, but it just came out as a whimper as I reached out my bloodied hand to them.

"Morrison," Duncan said to the healer as he helped Will off the floor. "Can ye sit with Lady MacLeod for a bit?"

"Aye, sir! I am tending to her wounds. Take yer time."

"We will return in a moment," he said, leading a heartbroken William out of the bedchamber by the arm.

+++

I woke with a slight headache and blurry eyes. I could feel the bandages tight around my left wrist as I opened and closed my hand. My right thigh was also bandaged, and it hurt something fierce. The searing pain made me wince at the thought. As I became more awake, I sensed that there was someone sitting on the side of my bed.

"Laird Graham," I said, startled that his face was the one I saw this morning. I tried to sit up on my pillows but could not find the strength. My head was still in the fog of sleep and Master Morrison's draft.

"Stay where ye are, lass. Stay where ye are," he said, with his hand resting on my shoulder. I looked at him and said nothing. "Word came to me that ye have had a hard time coming back home."

He was so calm and quiet that he broke my heart for him to see me this way. I was tired, and I was ashamed. I thought about what to say and with all the honesty I could muster for a man I love and respect, I finally

8

said, "I have had a hard time coming back to *life*, my laird. Not just Dunmara."

He looked at me with the love and concern a father would as I continued with tears in my eyes, "Part of me died on a flagstone floor in Edinburgh the minute my bairn did." I shook my head and released the tears behind my eyes that fell upon my cheeks as I continued with my confession. "I have smiled, and laughed, and tried to forget what happened to me. But here I am before ye the broken vessel I did not want others to see me as."

"Och, my darling lass, yer not broken," he said, holding my hand. "Wounded, aye! But *not* broken."

I held his hand in silence and welcomed his calm comfort.

"What does causing harm to yerself by not eating or cutting yer flesh give ye, lass?"

I just looked at him with tears in my eyes for the shame of the actions I have taken and the fact that he is asking me this very direct question. I do not know how I can find the words for him, as I felt every hot tear land on my cheeks.

"Alexandra, my dear, I make no judgment on ye. I ask this with respect to ye. Just to better understand, aye?"

"Aye, sir." I thought about the words I said to Will and looked him in the eyes, raised my chin, in defiance of my own uncertain emotions, said plainly, "It gives me *control*."

I could tell my words shocked him, but he asked the question. He deserves the answer.

"Control of my own body and mind," I said, thinking it all through as I said the words. "*Control* of a body that willingly became that of my husband's on our wedding night and unwillingly that of Allan Calder when he took me on the floor by force in my father's house. *Control* of my mind that had been given willingly to thoughts of love, friendship, and family over the last several months, more so than I could have ever imagined," I said smiling through my tears and thinking about the men in my life and the new friends I made in the city. "And *control* of a mind unwillingly sinking every day into the depths of the crippling pain of loss and fear that willna leave me. I am *afraid* still there are still so many things I cannae *control* and it troubles me. It pains me."

I looked at him as tears streamed down my face. In the return to Dunmara, I drank too much, ate too little, and hurt my own body. I was in *control*, but in very negative ways, yet there was power in making these decisions for myself.

No one else can hurt me if I hurt myself first. That is the only control I have.

"Och, my darlin' lass," he said, wiping the tears from my face. "Ye have helped me understand yer thinking, and I only ask that ye lean on me, Duncan, and William. I believe we have our limits... as all men do," he said with a brief and sympathetic smile.

I smiled weakly back at him. I breathed in at his words as the tears ran down my cheeks at the thought.

"Ye willna find any men—anyone—on these clan lands who love ye more. We will try to support where ye need us to. Ye just might have to tell us how at times. But I promise ye, we will do what ye need... what ye ask of us. Ye have my commitment to that!"

"Aye, sir," I said softly. He held my hand as my eyes faded before me in tears and my own emotional exhaustion.

+++

The next time I woke, I heard the door open and saw Master Morrison standing beside the bed. He looked much younger than I remembered, but he was always very handsome. He stood out on the MacLeod lands because he was very fair with his light skin, long blonde hair that he tied back, and bright green eyes. He had a serious look, much like Master Harmon, and I suppose, for the same reason—he took his responsibility seriously and was committed to doing good for the clan he served.

Unlike previous healers, Master Morrison had also proven restraint on drafts and tonics that dull the senses. His approach is very much tied to the use of herbs and that sometimes nurturing the ways a human mind and body can mend themselves. Despite that, his last draft made me tired and weary.

"Master Morrison."

"Lady MacLeod, I wanted to see how ye were faring, but I didna mean to interrupt yer sleep."

"I am fine, sir," I said, trying again to sit up on my pillows. "I fear I have been here in this bed much too long, though. Yer draft may have been too strong."

He said nothing but helped me sit up and even put another pillow behind my back. "There, is that better?"

I just nodded in agreement to him. I was glad to be sitting upright.

"If ye wouldna mind, I would like to look at the bandages on yer arm and thigh to see how the cuts are healing. I am prepared to change the dressings fer ye."

I nodded again and offered him my arm first. He took out fresh linen from his bag to replace my bandage and a small jar of salve made from

St. John's Wort. He worked in silence for the most part. Our eyes met each other on occasion, and then he finally said, "They look just fine. Ye may have small scars, but they are not deep and will fade over time. Let us check the thigh, shall we?"

I pushed the linens down for him and pulled up my shift just enough to expose the bandage on my thigh. I said softly, "I admit this one hurts the most."

"I should expect it does! It is much deeper than the others and the newest wound. But let us see how it is healing."

I am not a healer, but I would guess that my attempts to reopen the original wound with my own hand made a bad cut even worse. Master Morrison applied his salve and gently replaced the cloth bandage.

"This one will take more time to heal, but I see no signs of inflammation that cause me concern—just the natural course of healing. If ye bathe, ye need to pat it dry and reapply this salve, and a clean cloth. I will leave both fer ye. If ye see any inflammation oozing from it or feelings of burning or fever, please call fer me. It will just take some time to heal, and I am afraid this scar may remain visible to ye."

"I thank ye sir, yer verra kind."

I thought about Will's words in Edinburgh that we all carry scars—some ye can see, and some ye cannae. This one I will carry forever.

"If I may ask ye, Lady MacLeod..."

"Please sir."

I have nothing to hide from our healer. In fact, this incident aside, as Lady MacLeod, it is important for us to support each other. He has a role in care of this family and this clan that is most important. Trust between us is essential on these castle grounds.

"Do ye have someone to talk to about... the reasons ye have taken such actions on yer own body? Yer husband, uncles, or Father Bruce, perhaps?"

I breathed in and said, "Master Morrison, I understand yer question and I appreciate yer reason for asking it as our healer. Like I said, yer a kind man."

We sat silently for a moment before I could find the words to tell another and worried at the same time that repeating the story would only cause me more pain.

"I will keep the story simple, sir. I was attacked in Edinburgh."

Before I could finish the statement, he took my hand and said, "I am so verra sorry!" I was slightly shocked at his hand taking mine, but appreciated his genuine care and empathy. Two important traits for a healer. Here is another man trying to support me in the best way he can, and it is a comfort to me.

"I thank ye, but the attack from another man resulted in the loss of a bairn. The man who did this is known to us and was never caught to pay fer his crime, so he haunts me every day."

He put both hands on top of mine now and said, "I cannae imagine such a thing! Such a *dreadful* thing, my lady!"

"It has been difficult fer me. Obviously. I told my husband and Laird Graham that I could not completely understand it, but I believed that if I hurt myself, I could lessen the fear of that man hurting me again. I ken that my words dinnae make much sense, but the haunting ghosts of pain often dinnae make sense."

"I wish I had a salve or a tonic for painful memories," he said thoughtfully and holding my hand tight, "but I do believe that the more

13

ye talk about it with others, the less ye have tormenting ye from the inside. The less ye will feel *alone* in the pain ye feel. Yer *not* alone Lady MacLeod! If I have learned anything in my time here at Dunmara is that ye have many people surrounding ye who love ye and only want the best for ye."

I smiled at him and thought about such a notion of releasing what was tormenting me against sharing with others, and the thought of Master Garrick's words about making a choice to find hope. Perhaps he is right. The more you talk about the pain you feel with those that love you, the more you can lean on them and not torment yourself.

+++

I woke again to only find another visitor walking into my bedchamber.

"Father Bruce," I said, trying to sit up again. "Please do come in, sir."

"I didna mean to wake ye, Lady Alexandra."

"Ye didna, sir. While I am confined to this bed and this bedchamber, I have had many visitors today."

He sat on the edge of the bed next to me and said, "I wanted to see if I could bring any comfort to ye through prayer or if ye needed to talk."

"I think a prayer would be comfort enough, this day."

With this, he could fulfill his obligation and I could spare myself from telling the story of the intruder again.

"Aye," he said as he placed his hand on my forehead, as I closed my eyes to receive his words and his blessing.

"Lord God, our Father, look with favor on our Lady MacLeod who is suffering. Release her from the pain she carries and grant that she sees improvement with

each passing day. Fill her with the faith and perseverance she asks for in her own prayers. Increase her assurance of Yer love, for salvation and healing belong to Ye. Strengthen her and grant that she may enjoy the blessings of abundant health. I pray this in the name of Jesus Christ, our Lord. Amen."

"Amen," I said as the tears formed in my eyes. His words touched me. They were words of hope for the future, and I valued each of them.

Father Bruce released his hand from my forehead and took my hand in his. He smiled at me and said, "Ye are surrounded by love and prayers, my lady. If ye accept the *hope* and *grace* of both, ye will find yer strength return to ye."

I could not speak for the emotion I had and just nodded to him in agreement. He was reminding me once again of Master Garrick's words about choosing to hope but now the acceptance of hope offered by those that only want the best for me. I am not alone in finding the peace I seek... the peace I need. I just need to accept the hope I am offered in abundance.

Father Bruce left the room as quietly as he entered. I closed my eyes and fell back to sleep in an instant.

+++

I heard the door open, and the person did not move or say a single word. "I am not turning around, Duncan," I said, lying on my side with my back to the door.

"How did ye ken it was me?" he asked as he shut the door behind him.

"Because ye always enter a room and wait to be acknowledged."

"I dinnae ken that! Do I *really*? That is *interesting*."

"That is *annoying*," I said under my breath, but perhaps just loud enough for him to hear my words.

He ignored my judgment and sat down on the bed next to me. "I just wanted to see how ye were, lass."

"I am *fine*."

"Ye *sound* it."

After a moment of silence between us, I turned over and said, "Why did ye go to Laird Graham? With all the poor man is going through, ye had to tell him *this*?"

"*Alex...*"

"I could have tried to solve this with my husband, but no! Ye had to tell your brother that as he struggles with his own health that his successor is struggling herself. I am *disappointed in ye*."

Duncan reacted only slightly to by rebuke and said, "I went to my brother to help Will as much as ye. I felt like yer husband's worry and fear sounded like anger to ye and I could see it in yer face with every word he said to ye last night. It broke my heart to see ye so! Ye needed calmer voices around ye, and Will needed calming himself. I kent that Laird Graham could do better at that than I could."

I could not argue his point, but I still hurt that the laird had another burden to bear... and I was that burden. "I just dinnae want him to worry fer me."

"Graham loves ye as his niece and the daughter of his heart. He will always worry fer ye."

I smiled briefly at his choice of words from the meeting with the Fine. Laird Graham is one of my last fathers and he does love me. I know that. I know that Duncan does as well. As angry as I want to be with him, he went to his brother because he loves both me and Will. It hurt me, but I understood why he did it.

We sat silently for a bit until my uncle finally said, holding my hand, "I hope he brought ye comfort, lass."

"Aye! Laird Graham always does."

+++

When I opened my eyes again, I saw Will's face before me. I smiled, as he kissed my lips before asking, "How are ye, my love?"

I put my hand under his chin and kissed him again. "I am better. I am glad ye are here. Please stay with me."

"I will *always* be here fer ye," he said as he wrapped me in his arms. He held me tight in his warmth and tenderness, which, along with the last of Master Morrison's draft, lulled me back to sleep once again.

+++

Difficult weeks passed. Things became better in some ways. The cutting of my body was the easiest to stop, with no blade at my immediate disposal. I also did not want to revisit the pain I had in my thigh. That wound was determined to torment me as long as it could in healing, which served as a deterrent in itself. I still catch myself running my fingers over the scars on my arms when I feel nervous or anxious, but I have not tried to make new wounds. For that, I am thankful.

Eating has been difficult for me. I eat as much as I can bear and feel Will's hand on my leg or caressing my hand under the table throughout meals for support. I am glad he is here, but I know he is still afraid for me. Despite his initial declaration that he would feed me himself, he has never pushed me in any way about food. His encouragement has remained silent and positive. At every meal, I keep negotiating with myself and playing games with my plate.

If I eat this, then I do not have to eat that.

If I move it around enough, it becomes cold, and I do not want it.

Or the excuse I use most often—*surely that is enough for today.*

Missus Gerrard also never said anything to me, but she has provided broth everywhere, including in our bedchamber each night. My weight has not returned fully, but I can tell I no longer feel weak, and drink is not knocking me out in an instant. I have also regained my energy to lay with my husband. I have not been able to regain my love of bread and butter just yet, but I hope that one day I will. And I think that I might know I am fully better when I finally ask Missus Gerrard to add fried ham and tatties to our breakfasts.

At the main table one evening, Duncan said to me, "How are ye both?"

"We are healing, sir," Will said with a quick smile to me.

"And how are ye this day, Duncan?" I asked my uncle.

"Aye, verra fine. Will," he said with a smirk and a nudge to the man's ribs, "I heard a lot of *healing* as I passed yer bedchamber last evening."

"I cannae believe ye would say such a thing," I said as I hit the man on the arm from behind Will. "*Shame* on ye, sir!"

Duncan had no interest in my admonishment or my embarrassment, as he stood up from his chair, grabbed his drink and walked away, shaking his head, and mocking us both.

+++

"Can ye believe such improper talk from Duncan?" I asked Will as I wiped my face from washing in the basin and started taking off my skirts and throwing them angrily at the chest sitting at the foot of our bed.

"Ye cannae talk to the men like ye are one of them and then act shocked that they talk to ye like... *yer one of the men*," Will said, taking off his breeches. "That starts with Duncan. Though I admit that am not sure how much drink he had this night to say such a thing."

"That is fair," I said as we got into the bed together, "but I dinnae need my own uncle talking of me... of us... and what we do here in our own bedchamber *that way!* I found it embarrassing, and it was in poor taste to say such things at the head table!"

"My love," he said as he grabbed my hips and rolled on top of me placing his knee between mine, "we are newly married, *everyone* is talking about what we are doing in this room, whether they can hear it or not."

"Stop it!" I said as he ran his hand up my leg and tried to kiss me. I turned my head from his mouth and started squirming beneath him and yelled, "Get *off* me!"

I am trying to make a point and Will is clearly trying to make another. He caught my mouth and kissed me, and I almost gave in for a second as it is so easy to do with him, until he said laughing, "Do ye not ken that everyone in the Great Hall kens what married men and women do together in their bedchamber?"

He was shaming me, and I wanted no part of it. He started to lift my shift, and I said, still squirming underneath him in resistance, "Get *off me*, Will!"

He stood up on his knees and released me by raising his arms above his shoulders. He freed me, but he was not fully moving out of my way. I had to crawl away from him on my back by my elbows and pushing away with my feet. My eyes were afire having to do so. He was making me irate! Will let me get just far enough away to think I was free before he jerked me back to him by my knees and raised my hips to his.

I screamed, "Will!"

"Och, aye! Scream my name!"

"Stop it!"

"Louder would be better," he said, now instructing me softly in my ear.

Now this is a battle of wills. Feeling better and more myself, I was not about to give in... not yet! I took the opportunity and my newfound strength to flip him on his back as I sat astride him.

My long, curly hair dangled above his face. He seemed shocked at the change and brought his hands to my hips and around my backside and said louder still, "Aye, my lady!"

I tilted my head and just gave him the look of disapproval he has already seen more than once tonight. I could not ignore what his hands made me feel.

"Are ye asking me to be the noisemaker then?" he asked me in a whisper.

"Will, I said *stop this display! Stop!*"

He yelled as loud as he could, "Och, my lady! Do that again! Ye ken how much I want ye! Touch me right there! Och, right there!"

Now he was taking this spectacle too far. I hit him in the arm as he yelled in response, "Harder! Harder!"

I put my hands over his mouth to silence him, and he kept up his act with loud grunts and moans under my hands and my hips.

"William Lachlan MacCrimmon, I said stop!" I said to him with my hands still over his mouth, trying my best not to laugh at his audacious display.

But he paid me no mind and kept up his act—for me and anyone listening.

He kept trying to pretend that I was ravaging him and made his moans and groans louder than he should have. His exaggerated movements nearly tipped me off the bed and onto the floor. I tried so hard not to laugh at one point.

"Ye sound ridiculous, man!"

I turned my head to him and gave another look that he should stop his dramatic show of love. He called my bluff and flipped me over on my back this time. "Och, lass," he said, kissing my neck.

He whispered in my ear, *"First, ye ken that I love it when ye say my full name. The other thing ye need to ken is that if all of Castle Dunmara isna hearing us, then I am not doing my duty to ye as yer husband. If ye wouldna mind, I dinnae want that reputation."*

I was getting weak with the fight and desire, so I kissed him as he kissed me earlier and showing my resistance was no more.

"My only ask is that ye not hold back," he said in my ear.

I just nodded at him in agreement with his instruction, and I met the passion he laid on me with my body with the loudest voice I could in return. At that moment, I no longer cared who heard us at Castle Dunmara or on the Isle of Skye.

+++

TWO
The Lambing

Dunmara Castle
Isle of Skye, Scotland
April 1767

Our arrival back at Dunmara was in time for a portion of the lambing season. While the year is usually marked by the influx of the lads for the summer shearing, the lambing season is critically important to the clan and one that often requires everyone to pitch in to help the crofters and shepherds.

For me and Auld Knox, it also helps us keep a current count of how many heads the crofters have for assessing the rents, prepare for the next shearing, and estimate potential meat and wool output in the coming year. This is another important time that can determine the ultimate success of the clan.

For me personally, it was always a welcome sight to see the newborn lambs scattered across the lands and fields each Spring. It was a mark of new beginnings and even a mark of the health of the clan.

Will walked into our bedchamber and said, "Love, I have to go help Roderick MacLeod. He came into the stables, looking for some additional help from Master Knox. He has a number of ewes about to give birth, and the majority are first-time mothers and he cannae be at multiple places at once."

"Well, let me go with ye, then," I said. "Perhaps another pair of hands could be useful. Laird Graham always said that I should learn more about this entire process fer the year, anyway."

"Then it may be good fer ye," he said before kissing me and helping me with my cloak. *"And I can keep an eye on ye."*

"Ye need to keep an eye on me, do ye?"

I kissed him and held him tight in my arms.

"I never like to be too far, that is a fact. Let us go. We can ride together, love."

+++

We were directed to the top corner of the field before the castle gates, as at least two of Roderick's ewes were, in fact, in active labor at the same time here. One was close, but not yet presenting. Roderick was already dealing with others closer to his croft and trying to ride back and forth. From what I could see, his current help was primarily young lads with little experience. He was clearly overwhelmed at the moment.

William impressed me instantly. He took immediate control of the situation and instructed me and a young lad of about ten years old on what to do for the ewes in our care this afternoon.

"Help move yers, Alex. She is a little too close to this mother, and she isna in labor yet. I am certain they want to help each other in their distress, but if the ewe smells the scent of another newborn, she may reject her own."

The lad and I struggled to help these poor mother-to-be move, but she did finally follow our urging and pulling to give adequate space between them all.

Will's ewe delivered first without any real help. She did beautifully. We all cheered and celebrated her birth. Will quickly stuck a small piece of straw up the nose of the babe. The wee lad sneezed instantly and began to breathe on his own. He rubbed the lamb's ribcage with the hay to get him going fully, and it was an absolute miracle to witness. It made me think about the gift of life and made me love Will even more. He was so loving and tender with the ewe and the lamb. I already knew it, but he proved once again that he would be a sweet and loving father.

He stood up quickly to check our ewes and then came back to his babe as he said, "Look here, it is important to make sure yer ewe is done and doesna have another babe. Then ye need to let her claim her babe and clean him. Then ye need to move her either to clean land or hay to keep them both safe. If ye have to force the lass to move, then do so. It will keep them both healthy."

"Aye," the lad and I said again together.

"It may happen naturally, but more often than not, ye will have to help the babe find their way to nurse and they need to soon after ye clear the mother to clean ground."

He carried the babe low and said, instructing us further, "If ye have to help guide the babe, carry it low next to her, so the mother can see it and follow ye with her eyes."

"Aye," we said together again.

Will tickled the wee lamb under the tail and said, "This will make the babe want to suck."

The lad and I watched the sweet babe go right for his mother's teat and suck as he properly should. He was an absolute darling and while he had a little prodding, knew what to do in an instant. I smiled, thinking that both mother and son would be healthy and fine. It was a blessing to witness, and it made me so proud.

Will and the lad helped the next ewe. My wonderful husband helped guide him again on what to do during the whole process. He impressed me with his knowledge, but I loved watching him help the wee lad. I stood there, beaming at him. This was a new skill I had not seen until today from him and it was so charming and loving.

"Will, my ewe seems in distress. She keeps getting up and down. I cannae calm her and dinnae ken what to do fer her."

"It is difficult to be sure. Let me see her fer myself."

He walked around, lovingly assuring the lass about his presence and that he was no threat to her. He was here to help her. I tried to stroke her head as he assessed the situation. Finally he said, "Aye, she is in labor. I need to ken if she has multiple babes. That could be part of her desperate struggle. Sometimes they can get in each other's way."

The wee lad and I watched him assess the poor ewe in distress by placing his hand gently inside her.

"Alex," he said softly to me. "I dinnae think there are two. The babe may be dead. Something is wrong. I will have to help her and help pull it from her if she continues to struggle to push. I dinnae want to lose them both."

"Do it! Do what ye need to save her... and the babe, if ye can, Will!"

We have had our own losses and I could not bear another. It pained me for a moment to think that my ewe was likely struggling with loss, much like I had. I watched my beautiful husband treat her with care—his loving care. He tried to give me the same care in Edinburgh, and I refused to accept it at first. I can see now how even the mundane tasks like brushing my hair, or talks before the fire, were his attempt to comfort and care for me. He tried to tell me that he was no threat to me, and I did not accept him. It broke my heart to see him in this moment work so valiantly to save this babe and his mother.

I stood looking at another gorgeous newborn lamb that looked so peaceful before us. Will was correct that the babe had died at some point. She looked perfect and soundly asleep upon the ground. No straw or rubbing of her body would wake her.

"Och, Will," I whispered, with tears in my eyes, looking at the dead babe lying still upon the ground.

"All is not lost, love. It is part of life fer the crofters. There will always be losses of lambs or ewes during this time. I am certain that if the man has babes with no mother, he will help a childless ewe adopt one and nurse. There is a process, but he willna want to lose a motherless lamb fer starving."

I nodded to him but said nothing. Will could certainly see the pain behind my eyes as I just turned silently for home on my own. When he was done telling the young lad what to tell Master Roderick about the loss, he walked with his horse all the way back to the edge of the stone wall before the castle behind me.

"Alex!"

Will called to me more than once and I ignored him. I walked straight ahead for only one destination. The only destination that could give me the peace needed. He called to me all the way to Cairn's Point, where I sat myself before the rocks memorializing many, but specifically my mother, brother, and father. I heard him call to me along the way through the gates, past the stone wall, and to the cliff. I could not say a word back to him. I could not even look at him. It was not his fault, but I could not!

"Alex," he said again before holding me tight above the promontory as I sobbed into his chest and rubbed the scars on my arm behind his back.

When I could finally speak, all I could say was, *"How?"*

"My love, please."

"No! Will! How can nearly every ewe on our lands have a bairn and I cannae? And then today, the ewe I was responsible fer lost her own babe. My heart broke fer her in that field."

"Please! Ye cannae think that!"

"I feel like am I cursed! I can only birth *death*. I didna want to feel it but, I do feel *broken*. I feel like I cannae give us what we want so desperately and that my poor mother today had the same fate because she was assigned to me."

"Och! Dinnae say such things!"

"Ye cannae say anything that will mend my broken heart, Will!"

"My love..."

"Ye can say *nothing! I am broken!* I ken ye are trying to comfort me, *but dinnae!* Not now! Just hold me and let me grieve fer us both and the poor wee lamb we just lost."

Will hung his head in resignation and held me tighter. He could not say anything that would mend my broken heart and as much as I hated to admit it, I knew that I could not mend his own.

+++

A fierce storm from the sea was lashing the castle. The lightning and thunder were more than I had heard here on the coast in a long time. Will wrapped his arms around me as I shuddered with each clap of thunder.

"Dinnae worry! The storm is passing, love."

"How can ye tell?"

"Count the seconds between the flash and the thunder that follows. That tells ye how many miles away the storm is. I can already tell the time is getting further apart."

With the next flash, we began counting quietly together, "*One, two, three, four...*"

Will held me tighter, and the next count we made together was to six. The thunder softened as the storm retreated, and the wind and rain slowed. Both were no longer violently lashing the sea-front windows of Dunmara.

"The storm is so unlike Glenammon," I said, smiling for a moment, remembering our first night together and a thrashing gale that scared me so and left me shivering in the cold of my bedchamber. "But I have not seen lightning like this in a long while."

"Aye, it is fierce, but like ye said, not having trees near the house makes a difference."

Tonight's storm was fierce, but did not seem to scare me as much as the one at Glenammon House. Perhaps that was the comfort of being safe in this bed with Will and inside the sturdy and safe walls of Castle Dunmara.

"Aye," I said in agreement before we fell asleep.

At some point, I looked at Will, who was clearly asleep and softly snoring on the pillow next to me. While the poor man has endured my restlessness in bed since we married, his snoring was a comfort to me because it meant that he was truly asleep.

He often found a way to curl himself into the small of my back in the night. I thought to myself that this giant man in sleep suddenly looks like the little boy crouched under the kitchen table hiding from his father. It was the sweetest thing.

I turned, put my arms around him, and brought him closer to me. I whispered into his ear, hoping he could hear me in his sleep, *"Ye are safe and loved, my darlin' man! Sleep well."*

+++

THREE
A Case For Education

At the back of St. Margaret's chapel, in the area that was designated for the school, I walked in to find Master Harmon seated at his desk.

"Master Harmon, if I may interrupt yer work," I said, looking at the desks in the small room as I walked toward him.

He looked up from his papers and said, "Of course, Missus." He immediately corrected himself and said with a genuine smile, "I apologize, of course, Lady MacLeod. Forgive me, I am continuing to learn."

"Master Harmon, I am sorry we could not meet sooner, as ye must know I have been in Edinburgh settling the estate of my late father when ye arrived here at Dunmara and have had much to do since returning. The lambing season has been a focus for the clan."

The man knows nothing of what happens during this time of year or how difficult my return to Dunmara has been for me. But it is time to return to my responsibilities here as Lady MacLeod.

I heard myself being more formal with my speech and almost laughed at my own arrogance trying to speak the King's English with a distinct Scottish accent. But the man nodded to me, so I kept up the pretense.

"I am Lady MacLeod, and I am sorry for your loss. Laird MacLeod has been most generous to offer me lodging within the castle grounds. Of course, I am not so ignorant to know that he has probably done this to save an Englishman from his own people *and* to keep an Englishman close."

"I hope ye are comfortable at Castle Dunmara, sir."

"I meant no offense, my lady."

I admired his honesty and his accurate assessment of the situation. My uncle made it clear that we needed to protect the man and from what I could tell at first, he was correct. This man needs protecting and, on the second point, I am not certain if I fully trust him.

"Master Harmon," I said, ignoring his remarks and moving closer to his desk, "how many students do ye have at present?" I could suddenly feel the power of my position and it made me stand tall before the man as I waited for his answer.

"I have eight."

"And the mix between boys and girls?" I asked, already knowing his answer.

"As I told ye at the celebration, all eight are boys. They range in age from six to ten."

I nodded my head in understanding that these were his words to me, but pursed my lips, signaling my displeasure all the same. If he did not get the message at the celebration, he did now. I knew what was coming in response, but this was not the answer I wanted.

"Did Laird Graham tell ye upon yer arrival that I had asked that we expand our education to the girls at Dunmara?"

"He did," he said honestly as he stood and moved in front of his desk to stand before me, holding his ground. "Laird MacLeod told me that he wanted us to draft a proposal and present it to him for approval together. I took that to mean upon your return. If I misunderstood, then I must apologize to you both. I have submitted my first draft to him, to get initial feedback from him. However, I welcome your thoughts on the draft, Lady MacLeod."

I was slightly annoyed that he acknowledged that we would work on this together, but had already submitted his own draft. "Well then, I will find it and read it so that I can give ye my *thoughts*. You should know that I have been clear that I believe that Clan MacLeod can lead here in the Western Isles and Highlands by educating girls."

He just looked at me as I said passionately, "I know what my education has meant for me, and every lass on MacLeod lands should have the same opportunity. Knowing how to read and write, at a minimum, can open a whole new world to a child, as I am sure ye understand. And with the ability to read, those that want to know more about the world of history, science, or literature, would be given the ability to learn more or explore, on their own, through books. We have just brought an assortment of books from Edinburgh to donate to the school, sir."

"Yes, your uncle Duncan delivered the books to me just this morning, but I have not had a chance to look at them all," he said, smiling at me. "At first my glance, I have to say it is an impressive collection of historical works that I will want to spend more time with. I cannot wait to read them myself and I know they will benefit the school and students considerably!"

We just looked at each other for too long and just as I felt breathless before him all of a sudden. I broke his spell and finally said, "Please see me and the laird in his chamber tomorrow after breakfast and before yer students arrive."

"Aye, I will join you both there," he said. I walked away and could feel his eyes on me, but I did not look back.

+++

"Are ye sure, love?" Will asked before kissing my cheek and then my neck.

"It is early, like the last time," I said in his ear, "but I have missed my courses twice now. I am afraid after... what happened, that we should not tell anyone else. I just wanted ye to ken."

"We just have the healer, Master Morrison, here," he said, thinking about our options for support.

"Aye, but we have Missus Gerrard. She also serves as a midwife at the castle. In fact, she has birthed most of the bairns on our lands, including me!"

He smiled at me and seemed relieved that I would be supported here at the castle. We were settled in bed reading. I secured Master Harmon's draft proposal from Laird Graham before he retired for the evening. He admitted that he had not read it as he waited for me to return and was uncertain why the man drafted it without talking to me. I told my uncle of our morning meeting, and he said that he trusted me to take the lead and would support me.

I sat in bed with Will as we were both reading. I suddenly stood up, throwing the parchment on the bed, as I said, "This is not a draft proposal on *how* to educate lasses. It is an entire discourse on *not* educating them!"

I was angry and disappointed. I was not looking for another battle to fight. In fact, I am not sure how much strength I have left in me at the moment for another fight. I sat before the fire, stroking the fading scars on my arm and thinking about how to overcome such opposition—such entitled, English, and *male* opposition.

Before long, William came to me. Sitting behind me now, much like he did at Glenammon House, he put his legs and arms around me and his chin on the top of my head. My anger and frustration were not just coursing through my mind, but throughout my entire body. He rocked me a bit to calm my emotions.

"Tell me about what ye asked Laird Graham about the school," he said, as he held me tight.

Immediately, I felt calmer. Still enraged at the fight ahead of me with Master Harmon, but calm and supported in my beloved's arms.

"I forgot ye didna ken because it wasna announced to the entire clan. In council before the Great Hall where we discussed the announcement of Master Harmon's new assignment, I asked to consider educating young lasses at Dunmara. I told my uncles how much it meant to me to be educated, and I saw an opportunity for Clan MacLeod to lead on the Islands and Highlands by opening our school to include girls."

"Aye! Being able to read books can change yer life and open up new worlds to explore and think on yer own."

"That is exactly my point," I said in agreement and proud that he understood the doors that can open, being educated himself. "Why should the man be so resistant to giving girls an opportunity to better themselves and explore the world through books, if nothing else?"

Will continued to rock me in his loving arms but said nothing.

"Will, ye already ken what worlds were opened to ye with a mother that could read and write. Can ye imagine what other opportunities may have presented themselves to say... Mary MacAskill if she had an education?"

"Love, dinnae lament Mary. Her fate was not of yer doing. I can tell ye carry the pain of her loss! Yer gift to Canongate Kirk told me as much."

"Aye, I do lament Mary."

Will rocked me a little, knowing that what I said was true and he was perhaps fearful that Mary MacAskill was another ghost haunting me. And she was. I never had to fear seeing her around every corner like Calder, but seeing her in such a state and then her death caused me a deep sadness that I could not explain. Perhaps it was intensified by my own loss in Edinburgh, but Mary's death hurt me. It changed me.

"Set yer anger and pain aside. How can ye convince the man to think in a new way?" Will asked, being the wise counsel I needed in this moment and still rocking me slowly, his hands across my own.

"I dinnae ken," I said, stroking his hands wrapped around me. I felt his strength and his support and thought more about how to convince a man entrenched in his own masculine and English thinking to do the right thing by the lasses on MacLeod lands.

When I did not answer, Will said softly in my ear, "*First, ye find the core of the man's resistance.*"

"Aye, and his writing told me some of that. It is partly due to his own English tradition and to what he calls the *economics* of education. That includes what he can handle and the reality of investing that *valuable* time in people—lads essentially—who can have further education. He seems to think that educating girls is a waste of his time."

"Then I ask ye again—*how* can ye convince the man to think in a new way?"

"I dinnae want to demand it as Lady MacLeod, but I might have to." I went silent again and finally said as the thought came to me, "Or... I may be able to convince the man financially."

"What do ye mean?"

"If I cannae convince him to take on lasses in his classroom on the honest and moral principle of it, perhaps I can convince him with the expansion of his purse. What is a better motivator than money?"

"Ye are becoming more of a clan chief, every day," he said, kissing the top of my head again.

Will's agreement emboldened me ahead of the meeting with my uncle. But more than that, he has proven once again that he is the valuable partner I need as clan chief and as a leader. Just as Laird Graham said, Will loves me for me, but makes me better. His gentle encouragement makes me stronger, and I try my best to feel that more and more every day we are back here at Dunmara. It is not always easy for me, but I want and need his help to be stronger.

+++

Master Harmon, as requested, met me the very next morning in Laird Graham's chamber.

"My laird, I appreciate yer early morning counsel. Let me get right to my request for this meeting so that Master Harmon can join his class. Before I left for Edinburgh, and we prepared to announce that we would have a new educator at Dunmara, I asked that ye consider the education of young girls on MacLeod lands."

My uncle nodded to me in acknowledgement of this request, but remained silent.

"This is an area where I believe Clan MacLeod can stand apart from other clans on Skye and the Highlands, but it is more than that. It is the right thing to do fer our young girls."

No one said a word, and I kept talking, "After my request, ye asked that Master Harmon and I work together on a recommendation for this plan."

"I did."

"We still owe that to ye, sir, but I read Master Harmon's initial draft and believe there is a *moral difference* in our thinking on this topic. Before we go down a path of trying to compromise, I wanted to discuss those differences together."

"Aye, Alexandra," he said with a smile and perhaps a little pride that I was taking the lead on a topic that I felt so passionate about. This is another chance for me to prove my leadership ability to him. I could tell Master Harmon was not happy being put on the spot, but he had made his opinion known by placing it in writing and it is a fair ask that he defend his position—even on the spot. We cannot work together on the *how* if we do not agree on the *why*.

"Master Harmon," I said placing his parchment on the desk before Laird Graham, "I read yer draft proposal and it was clear to me that ye are completely opposed to the education of girls and that yer opinion is based on the thinking that their education is almost a *waste of time* as they are destined to be nothing but *wives and mothers.*"

"Lady MacLeod," he said trying to correct himself before the laird and myself, "I meant that we need to look at the *economics* of spending time educating girls who have no hope of further education *not* just the roles they will have as wives and mothers that need no education."

He knew the mistake the minute he said the words, and with one look at Laird Graham, he did as well. He nodded to me to continue knowing that, with his approval or not, I was not likely to back down against fighting the man's thinking.

"I cannae think of a more important role than being a wife or a mother."

"I did not mean to offend using the words."

"Aye, ye did," I said back to him. He shot me a look at my admonishment, and I gave him a cold stare back. His thinking is not only offensive to me as a woman but also short-sighted. I have been tasked with thinking about the future and I am Alexander MacLeod's daughter.

We will find ways to be ahead of our time. That includes the education of girls, and I am not going to back down on this request.

"I think in any home on MacLeod clan lands that an educated *wife* is a help to her husband in running his household and that the children of an educated *mother* can become educated themselves in many ways before they ever arrive in yer classroom. So, if we are talking *economics* in that sense, Master Harmon, then an educated *woman* should make the role of an educator on our lands *much easier*. Should it not?"

Master Harmon was not happy, but he stood tall in his black coat and breeches and said nothing against my argument. My argument against his English bias.

"I welcome yer opinion as an educator, Master Harmon. Ye have a skill I do not, but I need ye to accept the ask and expectation here at Castle Dunmara. I am willing to work together—work with ye sir on *how best* to make the education of girls possible fer ye *and* the children. But we will no longer debate whether it is prudent to educate girls on our lands. Girls *will* be educated here. If that is not acceptable to ye, sir, then perhaps this is not the best assignment fer ye."

"I can accept this as yer direction, Lady MacLeod, but I am one man. And some of my arguments on *economics* have to do with the practicalities of the classroom. The more students we have at varying levels, the harder it is to give the children—boys or girls—the attention they deserve."

"That is a fair point," Laird Graham said, looking at me with a slight smile that told me he was certain I already had a response for this argument. It was also a leadership moment to acknowledge the man's thinking in this debate. He had every right to make this point. I had to acknowledge it.

"Aye sir, it is," I said with a smile, accepting this challenge. A challenge more palatable than not educating an entire population for no reason other than their sex.

I moved toward the man and said, "Master Harmon, what is yer wage? Twelve pounds a year?"

"Yes, Lady MacLeod, that is correct, including room and board."

"Then yer castle accommodations have ye ahead on that score," I said with a smile. But the man knows why he is in the castle as much as I do, and it has nothing to do with grand accommodations in honor of his position. I continued anyway, "What if we raised yer wage to twenty pounds a year, sir? Would that cover the additional work required for more students?"

Laird Graham did not stop me, knowing full well that we had the money for it in our own coffers, and that I could supplement with my inheritance to have influence—and to make my point—if needed.

I looked at the laird and he smiled at me, and said, "The lady has spoken, sir. What d'ye say?"

Master Harmon was shocked by this and said almost reluctantly, "Yes, I believe that is acceptable, Laird and Lady MacLeod. I agree with your terms. We can find a way to make it work for more students. I would like to better understand how many new students we expect and any other requirements ye might have, though."

The laird nodded at this, confirmed Master Harmon's new wage, and dismissed him back to his classroom, but not before letting us both know that we still owed him a recommendation on *how* we will do this.

I waited for the man to leave the room before saying, "Thank ye, my laird. I ken I was hard on the man calling him out on the spot in front of ye. But I needed to ken that he would move his thinking to make the plan work. I dinnae want to spend days on end debating the principle and not making any progress on yer ask."

"Aye, lass, ye did fine," he said, turning serious now, "but is this my ask or yers?"

"I have been insistent, sir. That is true! While I ken that I am passionate about this topic, the ask is yers as laird. Ye make the decisions on these lands, not me. I am here to help ye. Ye let me lead on a subject I feel passionately about, and I thank ye fer that. But the ask is yers and the approval of our plan lies with ye. It lies with ye alone."

"Do ye remember the advice Duncan gave ye about men with *thwarted ambitions*, lass?"

"Aye, sir," I said, remembering the talk with Duncan and my father the night before I was named heir and successor. "He told me that they can be a danger and that I should not give into my instincts to try to fight them."

I thought about how the words were even more true after Edinburgh and my foolish attempt at thwarting Allan Calder. I failed in this task once already. I do not want to fail again.

"I will also tell ye the same warning applies to men with *wounded pride*."

"I didna realize that was what I was doing."

He gave me a sly smile. Perhaps he was not convinced that I did not know what I was doing. In fact, my own words showed that I knew exactly what I was doing. As confident as I was defending my convictions before Master Harmon, I believe I may have just made an enemy out of the one man who can make my vision at Castle Dunmara a reality.

+++

I stood in the back of the room and listened to Master Harmon talk to the young lads under his instruction. He seemed to have an incredible ability to engage his students. He was more animated than I have ever seen him before in my own presence. He had always been so calm and reserved... so *English* as Will says.

I listened to him talk about the basics of the alphabet to the youngest and the reading lessons to the oldest. He adapted perfectly to the needs of each student to whom he was talking. I thought to myself that perhaps this is what is comfortable for him, to engage with the lads and that he does not feel he can be as open or direct with the lasses.

I will give him a nod to respect and decorum but will ask him about this approach honestly when we next talk. It is my belief that if he cannot treat them equally, our plan will never work. I do not want the lasses to feel less than or like they are a task and chore he does not want.

I slipped out of the room without talking to him and I could tell he also tried his best to ignore that I was there at all. My uncles were right. I thought a lot about the concept of *wounded pride* in my approach to working with Master Harmon. As much as I hate to admit it, I might have to temper my approach and protect the man's pride in order to bring him around to my way of thinking.

+++

Master Harmon and I spent many days working on our proposal. I could tell that he was still unhappy about being brought before Laird Graham in the manner he was, but he did not argue the finer points of educating girls with me. We still had work to do on negotiating *how* to educate girls on MacLeod clan lands.

Together, we determined that there were about the same number of girls as boys in the immediate area. We would start with the ones on castle grounds or closest to the castle. The ages were broader, as young as five and as old as thirteen. But not having the opportunity to learn prior, they are all at the same level and would begin with the fundamentals together. He freely admitted that this made things much easier for him. We agreed on the basics of learning English letters, how to write and sign their names, and eventually broader reading and basic math.

"Like yer lads, Master Harmon, I want these young lasses to ken that this is just the beginning fer them. With these basic elements, it can both instill confidence and open up further study, even if it is just a lifetime of reading and studying on their own. Though I admit, I hope that the view on education fer lasses expands across Scotland and England. They deserve every opportunity the lads have before them."

His silence and his stare were unnerving, so naturally I felt the need to keep talking.

"Master Harmon, my opinion is not just because I feel fortunate to have been educated. I have also seen the impact of *not* having an education on the life of a lass. Will ye permit me to tell ye a story?"

"Please! Please do, Lady MacLeod," he said as he turned to me anticipating the tale I had to tell. By all appearances, he seemed as if he actually wanted to hear what I had to say. I appreciated him being open to another point of view. I thought about my words carefully.

"There was a young lass on our lands by the name of Mary MacAskill," I said, thinking about the young woman that despised me as much as I did her for so many years. I still smiled slightly at the thought of the miserable lass and her insistence on being near the kitchen constantly, even though she did not work there. Aside from the love triangle with Jenny and Wesley, I could never understand why she was always in the kitchen—or why the notice of it caused her such anger.

"It is a long story, sir, but she wasna verra kind. In fact, many of us called her *Mean Old Mary MacAskill.*" Master Harmon laughed at the mention of her name, but let me continue.

"Mary left our lands with a lad who had been banished for transgressions against the clan." I could not tell him the full story and was thankful that he did not ask. I would have been embarrassed telling the tale to another.

"My uncle Duncan escorted him off of MacLeod lands, to never to be seen again. By leaving with the man, however, Mary took his same punishment. She, too, would never be allowed to return to her own family here."

"Oh my goodness! That seems harsh!"

"Aye! It was a severe punishment, but it was declared by Laird Graham and recorded. Mary arrived in Edinburgh maybe two months before we did. Soon after, the lad she left with got himself killed in a brawl outside a tavern near the docks in Leith. Mary was left to fend for herself, alone, in a crowded city she didna ken. The one thing she did ken was that she was left with no chance to find her way home. Mary had to sell her body and beg on the streets and taverns in Edinburgh just so that she could eat something or hope for a moment of shelter from the night air."

"I cannot imagine such a thing," he said, shaking his head at the thought of a young lass living alone on the city streets.

"The lass lived in the soot and the cold rain of the city on her own. We came upon her begging in a tavern, and it was a haunting sight. Sir, kind or not, to see the lass we knew from home here on Skye in such a state was painful to witness. Days after our meeting, she was found dead, floating in the Nor' Loch."

I paused for a moment to collect myself, as I did not want to be too emotional as I concluded the story. I wanted him to hear the lesson of it, not just a woman's emotional pain in telling it.

"Mary only knew how *to write her name*, Master Harmon. In fact, that is how we kent the lass died," I said with tears forming in my eyes lowered again at the thought of such a thing and perhaps in a silent prayer for Mary MacAskill.

"Mary had the foresight to stitch her own name in her skirts and her death was recorded in the papers. Had she not done that, she would have just been another forgotten in a pauper's grave without anyone knowing of her fate."

The man sat back in his chair at the story I had to share. I knew I was making my point, and I also needed to release my own thoughts on Mary MacAskill. She has haunted me for so long and I was going to do everything I could to turn that into a positive thing for me and for this clan. I tried first with my donation to Canongate Kirk before we left Edinburgh, but the school here is equally important.

"Mary and I grew up on these clan lands together, but our experiences were as different as they could be. I believe that she could have had a different life—or at least I *hope* she could have—if she had the same opportunities I did."

Master Harmon nodded to me, but still said nothing.

"First, because I believe she would have made different decisions at the verra start, and that she would have never been so swayed by the sweet talk of a man to lure her from the only home she had ever known. But also, because I believe that had she been educated, she could have done more when forced to *help herself* in the city. I do not know that for a fact, but I have *hope*. Who knows, sir? Perhaps her lack of confidence in not being educated added to her bitter and jealous nature all along."

Master Harmon looked at me and nodded his head slightly that this could have been Mary's thinking. I had not thought of that before I said the words to him that her insecurities could have fed her ugly treatment of others.

"I ken that I have not been faced with the hardships that Mary had or that many women across our Scottish or English lands have, but sir," I rose myself up and said with conviction, "I tell ye, that I ken well enough to believe that knowing nothing but how to write yer name, or to sew yer name in yer own skirts, surely puts ye at a disadvantage in this world."

He turned his head to me on these words and I looked him in the eyes as I said as the tears started to well in my eyes, "It puts ye in a place, as a woman, where ye have nothing to rely on but yer basic instincts and often that means yer body when forced to help yerself. I want all the young girls on our lands to ken that they can rely on their minds and their own talents. I want them all to have the chance that I have had, and that Mary did not."

Master Harmon looked at me and his face had changed. It seemed softer and his eyes were intense, as I finally took a breath and stopped talking. He touched my arm and said, "Then, including girls at this school at Dunmara, is a *mission* for you, Lady MacLeod."

I had not thought of it before, but I suspect he is right. It is a mission! And an honorable one at that! I stood up to leave as his hand fell from my arm. "Aye sir, it *is a mission*... and maybe even an atonement."

I walked away feeling breathless and emotional. I do not know why I feel so responsible for Mary MacAskill. But I do. She showed me nothing but ugliness and bitter resentment in her life, and I offered the same back to her in willing opposition. But the lass also showed me that we did not have the same opportunity in life, and she taught me a valuable lesson in gratitude.

I had an education, and Mary did not
I had money, and Mary did not.
I had the support of an army of men, and Mary did not.

I had a different life at Dunmara, but I knew nothing else. I was not completely ignorant to our differences, but it was not until Edinburgh that I saw the true inequities laid clearly before me. Her life was a lesson presented before me. It was a painful, but positive lesson in gratitude brought about by Edinburgh. One that I tried to rectify to the extent I could with my bequest at Canongate Kirk. But one that I had to take that lesson and try to make life better for another Mary here at home.

I am not certain if I was winded talking about the emotional story or if there was something about Master Harmon touching me. I am certain Will would not appreciate him being so bold. Either way, I hastened my retreat from the school.

I stopped at Cairn's Point before heading back to the castle to stare into the sea for hope and to calm my mind and my spirit. I am not sure if the churning sea and the bitter chill moved me inside, but I did not stay long before searching for the warm comfort of Will's arms before the fire in our own bedchamber.

+++

Laird Graham said proudly, "I approve this recommendation, Lady MacLeod and Master Harmon!"

I was beaming with pride that young girls will be educated on our lands. In our evaluation, we had Master Harmon in full agreement, and his new wage was put into effect as of this day.

"Alexandra, ye will work with the parents to prepare the lasses fer school and Master Harmon, ye will prepare for the expansion of yer classroom."

Master Harmon said, "I believe at the start I can share desks, but I may need more help on new desks and chairs in the future if the class grows. But we will definitely need more quills, parchment, and ink for the new students."

"Consider it done, sir," Laird Graham said. "I will lend to ye from my own stores until we can secure ye more fer the school."

"I thank ye both, but I have one more request," I said. They both looked at me confused, if not somewhat weary of my *requests*.

"I want wee Robbie to be in Master Harmon's class, my laird."

"Aye, but ye would have to talk to his mother and Master Knox, Lady MacLeod."

"If I have yer support, my laird, then I will. That means, Master Harmon, ye may have one more in yer class. My cousin, a lad of nine, kens enough sir, but he needs to know more than just the stables. My father has already paid for his education at the University of Edinburgh, and he has to have a better foundation than he does now fer that to happen."

Master Harmon nodded as my uncle said, "Ye can work that with yer aunt and Master Knox and then inform Master Harmon if he has a new student."

"I will await your direction," Master Harmon said as he nodded to us both.

Laird Graham said, "Master Harmon, in celebration of our agreement this day, I would like to ask ye to read a poem or other writing ye deem worthy fer us this night after supper in the Great Hall. Read two, if ye like, sir! I believe it is important to have ye before the clan, so they can see ye as welcome on our lands and so that ye can connect with others, including the parents of yer students."

The laird was right in his thinking, but I could tell Master Harmon felt uneasy at first on the ask and being put before a broader audience, especially after we announce that girls will be welcomed at his school.

Master Harmon just nodded his head and said, "I am happy to do as you ask, Laird and Lady MacLeod."

+++

FOUR
Making Amends

After supper, a weary Laird Graham stood up and spoke before the quiet hall. "I have asked our new educator, Master Harmon, to share a poem with us this night before we depart fer the evening. We all ken how important an education is, and I am proud to announce that he and Lady MacLeod drafted a plan that will open education to young lasses on our lands. We will start with those here on castle grounds and look to expand as we can."

The room started talking and some of the women began cheering and celebrating openly, signaling their own approval of this decision.

The laird winked at me and raised his hand to quiet the room to say, "We believe that this is important fer the *future* of Clan MacLeod and we are fortunate to have an educator that believes the same."

"If ye please, Master Harmon," he said, inviting the man to the front of the room.

The room became deathly quiet, but Harmon stood tall and said, "I thank you, Laird and Lady MacLeod. I look forward to the expansion of our classroom for the benefit of the clan. I am at your service, always."

It was an incredibly kind statement, and we both nodded to him in appreciation of his remarks and reverence. He was walked unceremoniously and perhaps reluctantly into this decision at the start, but I do feel like he has come to a genuine and willing agreement.

"I stand before you all this evening to recite *The Canonization,* by John Donne."

I looked at Will and he did not look back at me, but I knew that we both knew the love poem. I also knew it was long and could not believe he was not going to read it but recite it. He had no papers or books before him. This is a new and decidedly romantic side to Master Harmon I did not expect.

"John Donne was an English poet who wrote many a verse and even sermons over a hundred years ago. His words are revered around the world." Master Harmon took a deep breath and started the poem.

"For God's sake hold your tongue, and let me love,
Or chide my palsy, or my gout,
My five gray hairs, or ruined fortune flout,
With wealth your state, your mind with arts improve,
Take you a course, get you a place,
Observe his honor, or his grace,
Or the king's real, or his stampèd face
Contemplate; what you will, approve,

So you will let me love.

Alas, alas, who's injured by my love?
   What merchant's ships have my sighs drowned?
Who says my tears have overflowed his ground?
    When did my colds a forward spring remove?
      When did the heats which my veins fill
      Add one more to the plaguy bill?
Soldiers find wars, and lawyers find out still
   Litigious men, which quarrels move,
   Though she and I do love.

Call us what you will, we are made such by love;
   Call her one, me another fly,
We're tapers too, and at our own cost die,
   And we in us find the eagle and the dove.
      The phoenix riddle hath more wit
      By us; we two being one, are it?
So, to one neutral thing both sexes fit.
   We die and rise the same, and prove
   Mysterious by this love.

We can die by it, if not live by love,
   And if unfit for tombs and hearse
Our legend be, it will be fit for verse;
   And if no piece of chronicle we prove,
      We'll build in sonnets pretty rooms;
      As well a well-wrought urn becomes
The greatest ashes, as half-acre tombs,

And by these hymns, all shall approve
Us canonized for Love.

And thus invoke us: You, whom <u>reverend love</u>
Made one another's hermitage;
You, to whom <u>love was peace</u>, that now is rage;
Who did the whole world's soul contract, and drove
Into the glasses of your eyes
(So made such mirrors, and such spies,
That they did all to you epitomize)
Countries, towns, courts: beg from above
A pattern of your love!"

The Canonization, John Donne

Master Harmon was not only handsome, but also very engaging. His recitation was formal and deliberate. Using every bit of his English accent to reveal the words of Donne's poem, his delivery was filled with passion. I could see the women in the room lean in toward him as he spoke his words and felt the pull myself. At some point, Will took my hand in his and broke the spell of the man, not just telling the poem to the room, but to me. I know he could see my chest heaving above my bodice as I tried to catch my breath.

After people began to leave the Great Hall, I left Will with Duncan and Angus to seek out filling my glass from what remained in the jugs on the tables. I met a very proud Master Harmon on my journey.

"Well done, sir," I said as we touched our glasses together.

"Please walk with me as I seek to fill my glass again." I said, motioning him to a nearby table. I could not help but show him appreciation for where it was due. "Five stanzas of *The Canonization* and recited from memory, no less! Verra impressive!"

"I thank ye Lady MacLeod," he said, sipping his own glass and smiling. He was clearly proud of his accomplishment and the positive reaction from a room filled with Scots. "It is one of my favorite poems."

"I know ye were put on the spot earlier today, but how did ye settle on Donne as yer recitation this night?"

"Yer husband, madam," he said as I held my glass to my lips for a moment before finally taking a sip.

"My husband?" I asked, still unsure that what he said was correct and silently questioning why Will would say such a thing.

"Yes, Lady MacLeod. I asked Master MacCrimmon specifically in preparation for this evening and he said John Donne was your favorite poet."

I just smiled at him and looked across the Great Hall at a man whose eyes were locked on mine and not at all happy that I was talking to the educator on the side of the room alone. I looked back at Master Harmon with a weak smile and said again, "Of course."

Master Harmon moved in closer and said, "I wanted to try to make amends, Lady MacLeod."

He was close enough that I could feel his breath on my face, and my knees became weak. Not unlike what I felt when he was reciting his verse.

"I believe we got off to a poor start, and I wanted to show my respect for your position and your partnership with the school by reciting your favorite poet." Then he stepped closer again and said softly, "You have changed me with your passion for the school and you have helped me understand the importance of education for girls. Your story of young Mary touched me, and I am a better teacher for it. I am a better man for it."

I welcomed his honest admission, but I could feel Will's eyes still burning on me from across the room, and I took a deep breath. "I thank ye verra much for yer kind words, and I wish ye a good evening, Master Harmon. Well done, again! We must have ye do another recitation in the future."

I immediately returned to Will and held his hand in mine. Master Harmon seemed confused by my hasty retreat but was immediately met by others in the room, ready to congratulate him on his poem so he could no longer concentrate on me.

+++

As we prepared ourselves for bed, I could not think about how to talk to Will. I could tell by his sounds and sighs that he was as angry with me as I was confused by him.

We threw our clothes about. I placed brushes and mirrors down forcibly. He slammed drawers and doors and took extra efforts to pull back the linens and throw the pillows to the ground as hard as possible.

I refused to get in the bed and just stood next to his side and said, "I have no idea why ye are so angry, Will, but I can *feel* it."

He turned over on his pillow and looked at me and said, "Aye, I can say the same."

"I am *not angry!*"

"Aye," he said, almost laughing at me, "ye dinnae sound *angry—at all!*"

"Will," I said, sitting on the edge of his side of the bed with my hand on his chest, trying my best to calm him and maybe myself. "Talk to me, please."

"I dinnae like ye spending so much time with Master Harmon and..."

"And?"

"I saw the way ye looked at the man when he recited his *love poem*."

Will was not angry with me. He was jealous. I have to admit it made me happy in a way that he loved me so. I also respected him for telling me the truth of his feelings.

"I didna look at the man in *any* way!"

"I saw yer breasts heaving over the top of yer dress, as the man spoke in all of his *Englishness*! And he was looking at ye as he spoke his words! I saw him looking at ye directly! I am not blind, Alex!"

"Will," I said, trying to account fer the reaction he observed honestly. I cannot speak to anything Master Harmon did in the room. "The man recited a *love poem* from an *English* poet. Every woman in the Great Hall was reacting to the words in his accent and the emotion of the poem and his delivery of it... not the man."

He knew that the words I said were only partly true. I could not say what was happening between me and Master Harmon, only that I regretted that any sense of it had made my own husband unhappy. I love Will too much to risk doing something foolish to hurt him.

I reached to move his curls from his angry brow and cupped my hand around his face as I asked, "Why did ye tell Master Harmon that John Donne was my favorite poet?"

"He told ye then?"

"Aye, when I talked to the man tonight, I asked how he made the selection of the poem and he said ye told him Donne was my favorite poet. Why?"

"Why does the man care who yer favorite poet is?"

"He told me it was an attempt to make amends."

Will just looked at me with his eyes narrowed.

"Ye ken we started off at odds, but he has now seen the importance of educating lasses. That is a kind and respectful admission, is it not?"

He looked at me with a pained stare and did not answer my question. He remained silent in his own jealous anger.

"Will, it is innocent! Ye and I talked together in this verra room about how to convince the man to think differently *and he has*. This night was a celebration of expanding the school. Now... tell me, why did ye tell the man that John Donne was my favorite poet?"

He grabbed my hand from his cheek, kissed my wrist laden with old scars, and looked at me as his bright blue eyes went from angry to loving at once. "Because Shakespeare is *ours*."

His sweet admission took my breath away as I wrapped both of my hands around his handsome face before I kissed him as the tears formed in my eyes. With our foreheads together, I whispered, *"Aye, my love. Shakespeare is ours."*

+++

I awoke in the early hours of the morning and felt what I did in Edinburgh. I placed my hands between my legs and felt the warm blood of loss.

Delirious with grief, I backed away silently from the bed and found myself walking at dawn to Cairn's Point alone in my bloodstained shift, with streams of loss still running down my legs. I did not care how cold the morning air was, but just kept walking to my destination. I *had* to make it to the cairn.

At some point, Will came above the hill yelling my name. He found me carving two lines into the lowest rock of the cairn with another rock. Much like the cutting of my body, I was recording the unnamed losses I have endured as lines in the stones.

Unable to really speak, but holding on to him as I finally said quietly, *"I lost the bairn."*

"I ken, my love," he whispered as he gently took the stone from my hand and placed it back on the top of the cairn. He kissed my cheek and picked me up from the ground to carry me back to the castle.

I whispered Shakespearean verse back to him through my tears, *"There is a cliff whose high and bending head looks fearfully in the confined deep..."*

"Och, my darlin' lass!" he said, recognizing what I was reciting and perhaps wondering if he found me just before I put myself over the cliff. "Yer *so* cold. I have to get ye back to the castle."

Will carried me back to Dunmara and to our bedchamber under the watchful eyes of Duncan and Missus Gerrard, who met us at the top of the stairs. I can only imagine that they were all frantically looking for me, only to follow my blood-stained steps to the cliff. Missus Gerrard tended to me alone and in the same soft-spoken whispers Missus Malcom did in Edinburgh. I cried the entire time but said nothing coherent to her.

Master Morrison visited only to see if he needed to give a tonic for my nerves or for sleep and determined that he did not. I appreciated his restraint. I did not want another draft to make me sleep off and on for days.

When it was all done, Will held me in his arms and rocked me slightly against his chest as I cried. When he placed his hand on my empty belly and I put my hands on top of his, my tears immediately became sobs to the point that I could not catch my breath. He kissed the back of my head and my neck as he cried with me. I could feel his own warm tears fall on my shoulders and could feel in his touch that his broken heart matched my own.

"Please, dinnae cry. Please, ye ken I cannae bear it when ye do. Yer pain is my own and I am so verra sorry fer it."

"No, I am sorry," I whispered. I was sorry that I could not stop crying, and I was sorry to lose another bairn. But as much as I regretted that our hearts were breaking together again, I loved the man holding me, mourning with me, and comforting me.

As my tears slowed and I could breathe again, I asked softly, "Do ye think I am being punished for saying for so long that I never wanted to be a wife and a mother?"

"No. Dinnae think such a thing. I dinnae believe God works that way," he said. I turned around to him and wiped his tears from his face as he wiped mine with his thumbs.

I fell upon his chest and asked the questions I dreaded. The question that has haunted me as long as the man himself.

"Will, what if Calder hurt me more than Missus Malcom could understand? What if I cannae give ye a child and cannae have a MacLeod heir?"

"Och, my darlin'," Will said, hugging me tighter. "We are young, and havena been married a year. It will happen when it is supposed to. We will keep trying, aye?"

"*Aye.*"

+++

I woke the next morning to find Will before me, smiling his lovingly sweet smile and then kissing me tenderly.

"How are ye, my love?"

I did not answer his question as I honestly had no idea how I was feeling and just looked at him as he touched my face again.

"Christ! Yer burning up," he said, placing his hands on my chest and back on my cheeks and forehead. "I will call fer Missus Gerrard and Master Morrison. Ye have a fever."

"I am *so* cold," I said, wrapping myself in the wool blankets and shivering.

They both agreed that I likely caught the chill in the night air and that there were no signs of anything more serious with the loss that caused them concern. My runny nose and sore throat reinforced that line of thinking. I sat bundled up in the bed as the fire roared and wiped my nose constantly with one of Duncan's handkerchiefs that I must have confiscated on our travels across Scotland.

Missus Gerrard stroked my face and said, "Mi'lady, I will bring ye broth fer now and ensure ye and William can have yer supper in yer chamber this evening." She could tell I was worried about not being present at the head table and said, "Duncan can represent the clan this evening, Alexandra. Ye should stay warm and rest, try to sleep as much as ye can, so the fever can break. Ye will be better in no time, lass!"

+++

FIVE
Finding Our Way

I finally started to feel more like myself and decided it was time to leave my bedchamber. Honestly, I had been confined for long enough! I had become bored with myself and reading by the fire. I needed to get dressed. I needed human interaction beyond that of my husband.

I chose that my first task would be to talk to wee Robbie about attending school. I headed to the stables slowly, enjoying the fresh air for the first time in over a week. I could feel the color return to my own face walking across the courtyard in the fine sun and crisp air of the morning.

"Master Knox! How are ye, sir?"

"Aye m'lady," he said as he came to greet me with a tender smile, "I am verra fine. And how are ye?" For all of his rough edges, I suppose

Auld Knox is another father in my life. I could tell in his voice that his wife has let him know all that I have endured, and ever since my return, he has shown me nothing more that the genuine love and concern.

"I am better, sir. I thank ye fer asking."

"Yer here fer yer husband, then?"

"No sir, I would like to have a moment with wee Robbie, but I wanted to talk to ye first. Can ye spare me a moment?"

He seemed uncertain about my ask but said, "Follow me, m'lady. We can talk by the old stone wall near the paddock and watch Will break a new colt."

I waved to Will as we passed, and he smiled at me. He knew what I was going to ask the stable master and encouraged me to talk to the man here on his ground and not the lady's chamber out of respect for his position. This was not a discussion with the estate factor, it was a discussion with my stable master. The man's warm reception told me once again that Will was correct in his advice.

"Master Knox, like I said, I want to talk about wee Robbie. I hear the lad has done quite well for ye in the stables."

"Aye, ye ken Robbie is in the right place."

"I do. He is no longer splitting his time, then?"

"No. After ye left fer Edinburgh, Maggie agreed to release him to the stables."

I knew this was likely the result when the lad handed me the reins of Munro upon my departure. The boy did well that morning and impressed all of us in the courtyard—including the hardened and strict stable master.

"I would like yer permission again to split Robbie's time between the stables... and the school."

"School?"

"Aye sir! I want to find a way that he can do what ye ask of him, but also provide the lad time to begin his education with Master Harmon." Before he could speak, I continued, "I have talked to Auntie Sarah, and she agrees, but only if ye do."

"What were ye thinkin'?"

"Give the lad the morning in school and he is at yer service in the afternoon. This is not unlike what many of the children are doing. They are completing family chores before and after class."

"Ye asked me last summer to split his time wi' the castle and now ye want to split his time wi' school?"

"Ye are correct, sir, but I expect the school will close until the middle of August. I havena told Master Harmon this yet, of course, but I want to introduce Robbie to the idea and the expectations of education before that happens. He will split his time until school is ended and then he is all yours for the summer, only to return to that schedule when the school reopens."

He seemed to be thinking carefully about my words as I continued, "Master Knox, the lad has to be educated. Ye ken my father has paid fer his education at the University of Edinburgh."

"Aye, I do."

"I feel an obligation to ensure he is ready fer that, sir. This is about his future, *and ours.*"

As Master Knox has taken on more of his estate factor role and supported me, we have been focused on the future as partners to preserve this land and our way of life. He knows that this lad must have options and he would never say the words to me, but he knows that I have not produced an heir of my own yet. We may need to rely on Robbie.

"I can agree to that, m'lady," he said with a wink, "but yer gonnae have to convince the wee laddie."

"I ken my work here is only half done, sir! May I take the lad away to talk with him for a bit?"

"Aye," he said, pointing to the other side of the fence, "he is just there watching Will from the other side of the paddock fence."

"Thank ye, Master Knox! Yer a good partner to me, sir."

"And yer still a right pain in my arse, Alexandra MacLeod!"

I smiled back at him because I know this was Auld Knox's version of affection and I took every word of admonishment with the true love with which it was given.

+++

"Cousin!" Robbie yelled to me as I approached the other side of the fence. "Erm! I mean, my lady!"

"Och, my wee Robbie," I said as I ran my hands through his glorious auburn hair and kissed the top of his head over and over again. "I feel like I have not seen ye in ages!"

The lad has no idea what I endured over the last several days and why I had not been present at supper or visible on the grounds. Will came to the side of the fence and Robbie said, introducing me to the horse, "This is Thunder, Alex! Will is trying to train the lad."

"And how is Master MacCrimmon doing so far with this task?" I asked as I walked to the fence to kiss my husband.

Looking back into the face of a very embarrassed boy, we both smiled at him as he said flatly, "He's doing *fine.*"

"Well, then, that is good enough for his lady. Will ye walk with me, Robbie? Master Knox said it was fine to take a break from yer work for a moment."

"Aye," he said, but clearly unsure of why I was taking him away. He said as we walked away, "I will be right back, Will!"

"And I will be here waiting fer ye, lad," Will said with a reverent nod of his head. We all know who is running the training operations here at the Dunmara stables and it is Master Robbie MacLeod.

We walked all the way to Cairn's Point together and sat ourselves before the sea with the foggy mist rising from below. I breathed in the peace of the salty air and the sounds of the churning waves below.

Robbie said, "There must be a storm coming."

"Aye, the sea is starting to rage, isn't it?" I asked, already mesmerized by the flow of waves, the white-capped surge before us, and the rising sea mist. A storm was brewing, and we would have to be ready for it.

"I have to admit, I love it like this! There is the rhythm of the sea on a normal day, but the rage of a storm makes me happy."

We sat together for a moment watching the sea rise and fall together when I said, "Robbie, I want to talk to ye about school."

"School?" he asked, looking confused.

"Aye, I talked to Auntie Sarah and Auld Knox, and I want ye to start attending school with Master Harmon." He just looked at me as I continued, "Master Harmon is a good teacher, and I believe having an education can be important fer ye and yer life."

He remained quiet, so that only made me talk more. "Education has been verra important to me, lad. Ye ken Lady Margaret saw to it. Being able to read and study things I want to know more about has helped me. It will help me be a good leader for the clan." He nodded in understanding but still said nothing back to me. "Ye will learn to read and write along with other things like basic math, but those alone can be a foundation to learn about new worlds and new things in the future."

"Think of it, lad," I said, stroking his gorgeous hair and smiling at him, "ye would be able to *read* the letter I sent ye on yer own and ye could even *write* me a letter back in reply." He looked up at me in recognition of this fact and the argument seemed to register with him. "Aye! Would that not be special?"

He nodded to me in agreement, but still said nothing. I kept talking. "Ye can go to university and be a great man like my father! Ye ken yer uncle already paid fer ye to go to the University of Edinburgh, so ye need this basic foundation of education to do be able to do that, my love."

Robbie looked at me for a bit. Then, with a tear in his eye, and said, "But... I am not smart enough fer school!"

"Och! My darling lad," I said, wrapping my arms around him and hugging him tight, "why do ye think such a thing?"

He pulled away from me, lifted his hand to the back of his head and looked at me in pain from the memory of his injury, and said finally, "And I am blind in one eye."

"Robbie MacLeod," I said, scolding him slightly, but with love as I kissed the top of his glorious head over and over. "Ye are a smart lad and ye can learn to be even more so in school. Yer blindness will not stop ye, in any way!"

I ran my hands through his hair. For the first time, I noticed he was not squirming under my touch. In fact, it seems he seems comforted by it. He leaned into me as I wrapped my arm around him to hug him tight again.

Robbie looked up at me, still unconvinced, as I said, "I would like ye to start spending the first part of the day in Master Harmon's class and then ye are to return to Master Knox fer the last part of the day in the stables. Will ye try it fer me?"

"Aye," he said softly.

"I will take ye to class tomorrow and introduce ye to Master Harmon myself. Meet me after breakfast and I will go with ye."

"Aye, my lady."

"Robbie, look at me! Ye will not be doing this on a lady's command but my own, as yer cousin." He nodded to me as I said, "Should we go back and see if Will has made any progress with the mighty Thunder?"

The thought of returning to the paddock perked him up in a second as he leapt up and helped me up from the ground. We walked together back to the paddock, hand-in-hand.

"What do ye reckon, sir?" I asked Robbie as we watched Will talk and walk a much more disciplined horse than we saw just moments before.

"I think, like me, Will is in the right place."

He then ran from me and left me standing by the fence alone.

+++

At the head table, I looked about the room and thought about wee Robbie and his belief that his injury made him not capable of learning. His words broke my heart.

Will and I discussed it at length at the table. In doing so, we turned to each other, with our arms on the other's chair. We did not talk to anyone else or even noticing that we were in a room filled with other people.

"It isna just his injury, Will," I said. "I think the lad also believes that he doesna *need* to be educated to work in the stables. Even if the lad decides that university is not fer him, and he remains in the stables his entire life, being able to read and write will be important. Can ye tell the lad that ye are also educated?"

"Aye. Ye ken, love, that I am not as educated as ye, but I can read and write."

I touched his hand and smiled, "Ye are educated, my love."

"Ye ken that wee Robbie will do whatever ye ask of him?"

"I do, but I told the lad today that this ask to attend school with Master Harmon is not a command from Lady MacLeod, but my own as his cousin. I need him to believe in himself as much as I believe in him."

Will put his arm around the back of my chair and looked at me in my tearful eyes, and smiled. "Yer love fer the lad is a beautiful thing. I see yer love for others, and I feel yer love fer me, but the lad is special to ye."

"I will always love him," I said, smiling as he kissed me in front of the whole room as we remained in our own world. I could not say the words to Will, but sometimes I wonder if wee Robbie may be the only bairn I get to help raise.

+++

After breakfast, Robbie met me and dutifully walked to the school at the back of the chapel. His mother put him in a new coat for the occasion.

"I ken this is new fer ye, but I appreciate ye being so brave to try it."

He just looked up at me and smiled a weak smile. Much like wee Petey on his first day of school, I could tell the lad was nervous and still not convinced this was for him.

"Good morning, Master Harmon," I said, walking into the classroom at the back of the chapel much more cheerfully than I have before.

"Good morning, Lady MacLeod," he said, walking toward us with a welcoming smile.

"Sir, this is the young lad I mentioned," I said with my arm around wee Robbie. "Let me introduce ye to my cousin, Robert MacLeod. His mother and I believe it is time fer him to join yer class."

Master Harmon walked closer, shook Robbie's hand, and said, "I welcome you here to our class, Master MacLeod."

Robbie just nodded his head at the man, but still looked nervous.

Master Harmon leaned down to him and said, "Do you know any of your letters, young man?"

In a shaky voice, the lad said, "I ken my letters and can write my own name, but that is all. I cannae read, sir."

We both smiled at him as Master Harmon said, "Then, young man, you are already ahead of many in this class and have the foundation of reading *and* writing! I look forward to helping you learn more."

The boy stood tall and nodded again, as the room started to fill up with the other students.

"I will leave ye to yer schoolwork then," I said, making him look at me. "Robbie, may I join ye after class and walk with ye back to complete yer stable chores with Master Knox?"

He just nodded to me as I said, "Then I will see ye soon, lad."

+++

I waited outside the back of the kirk for wee Robbie. I hoped he had a good first day, or I was going to have a challenge on my hands for the boy to return for another. Just as the doors opened, I saw my beloved's face emerge from the door. He seemed happy as he ran for me.

"Och my wee lad," I said, hugging him tight and immediately putting my hand in his hair, "what do ye think?

"It was not as bad as I thought it would be."

"Will ye go back?" I asked as we started walking to the stables together.

"Aye, cousin! I ken my letters and can write my name, so I am not as far behind as some of the others in the class."

"That is right! And ye will learn a little more each day and soon ye will be able to read and write. Remember, ye will go to school in the morning and then the stables in the afternoon and if ye ever want me to meet ye after school, I am happy to. I will meet ye right outside the kirk and walk with ye."

"I like walking with ye," he said with a sweet smile and taking my hand in his.

I was touched by this and asked, "Then how about I meet ye every day after school this week and we walk back to the stables together?"

He smiled up at me and think he liked my company as much as the escort. I touched his glorious hair, and he broke away from me and began running to the stables once we crossed the courtyard. I stopped outside the paddock to talk to Will where he was still working with the mighty Thunder.

Will nodded to me and yelled across the fence, "How was the first day of school?"

"I think he will go back for a second," I said, smiling before he came to the fence to kiss me. I looked at him with loving eyes as I stroked his face. "Does that count as success?"

"I would say so," he said, smiling at me and then looking back to the lad, who was already knee-deep in mud and muck in the paddock.

"Robbie gained some confidence this day because he kens his letters and can write his own name, which is a lot more than many of the other students. I am proud of him for going because I could tell that the poor boy was *so* nervous this morning."

"Aye, the lad's confidence will grow. Give him time."

+++

Will held me in the bend of his arm and wrapped my curls around his fingers and he said, "I think about being with ye every second of the day. Even just like this, just being near to ye, holding ye in my arms or holding yer hand."

I smiled, thinking about the same. Just being near him made me happy. We sat in silence together for a moment and then he said, "But then there are days in the stables when I think of coming to yer chamber and taking ye over yer desk."

I laughed and turned to look at him over his chest and said slowly, "I appreciate being here with ye like this. I often think about the nights in front of the fire at Glenammon House, just holding on to each other and reading or talking. Those are precious memories that I will always treasure."

He smiled Down at me, remembering our betrothal and restraint as he stroked my cheek.

"And then, sir, there are days that I am in my chamber alone, thinking about ye coming from the stables to take me over my desk."

He laughed and then kissed the top of my head as he said, "We are of the same mind, my love."

+++

"This is a pleasant surprise," I said, greeting Duncan at the door to my chamber.

"Aye," he said. "I figured it was time to give ye an accounting of the brewery on Skye."

I sat down in the chair behind my desk, "Aye, ye have been verra busy with your new venture and I have missed seeing ye, uncle! But ye ken that the brewery and distillery are yer own, and ye owe me no accounting for yer work."

"I ken, but I want to share it with ye. It is going to be a fine operation, Alex!"

"I have no doubt!"

He sat silently for a minute in reflection and said, "I have been thinking about Alexander a lot with this project and let the lads building the place ken that I only want the best and most advanced materials for Glenammon."

"Aye, I confess that I have missed that copper bath every day since our return to Dunmara. I may have to task my husband to figure out how to make something like it here."

"And the cistern!" he said as we both laughed, thinking of how my father made his own homes advanced and modern by comparison.

"My father was ahead of his time. That is a fact!"

"He was and I want to make him proud, lass."

"And ye will! I would like to see your brewery when yer ready."

"That is why I am here! I would like to take ye and Will there tomorrow if ye can make the time for a ride out to the building."

At that moment, Will walked in the door, and I said, "Well, that is perfect timing! There the man is now!"

Will came into the chamber and shook Duncan's hand and I said, "Will, Duncan has made progress on the brewery, and he wants to give us a tour tomorrow. Can ye make that work with yer time at the stables?"

"Aye, that would be verra fine. I will let Auld Knox ken I will be away fer part of the day with ye both."

"Then it is settled! We will be happy to ride with ye to the new Glenammon brewery on Skye tomorrow."

Suddenly realizing that I usually do not see him here during the day, I asked, "Will, why are ye here?"

"Well, I thought we could continue the conversation we had the other night," he said, staring at me and willing me to remember.

"Och, of course," I said as I stood and walked around the desk.

"Duncan, if ye wouldna mind, this is... personal," I said, turning red at the thought. It was indeed *personal*.

"Aye, we can talk more at supper tonight and make a plan fer tomorrow," he said as he walked out of the door with a smile. I could tell he felt dismissed, and I gather the man knew exactly why by the look of anticipation on my face, but he said nothing to either of us.

Will came to me the minute the door closed, forcibly took my hair in his hands, and kissed me harder and with more passion than he has in a while. My husband has always been a passionate lover, but need and want are two different things and today I feel both.

He smelled of hay and sweat. I could barely stand he left me so weak, and his eyes showed me what he was expecting from me. I do not think I have ever wanted him more. I backed away from him slowly and with a sly smile said, "I believe ye said *over the desk.*"

"Aye, if ye wouldna mind," he said, smiling as he turned me around, moving my hair from my neck with one hand and the ink well and papers in front of me with the other. He placed each of my hands on the sides of the desk and bent me over as he bit my neck and shoulders and began lifting my skirts.

"Ye have my apology, my lady, as I have not paid enough attention to yer beautiful, round arse of late."

I could barely breathe as he hooked his hand around my right thigh and perched my knee atop the desk. He was not rough, but he was frenzied. I grabbed the sides of the desk as he took me with one hand tangled in my hair and his other hand forcing my hips to him. At the last, he bent himself over my back as we cried out for each other. We stayed still as we tried to steady our heartbeats and breaths together.

He said in my ear before leaving me, *"I told ye we would keep trying, but that was even better than I ever imagined standing in the stables thinking of ye."*

I turned to him, still trying to catch my own breath as he tied his breeches. I put my hands in his curls, wiping them from his forehead, and kissed him before saying, *"Aye! That may have been our best yet!"*

He held my hand as I walked with him to the door of the chamber and said loudly after he kissed me goodbye, "If ye ever need to talk again, sir, I am here in my chamber most days."

"I ken where to find ye, my lady!"

I could only smile with satisfaction as I watched my beloved man walk away from me and down the stairs to the Great Hall.

SIX
Glenammon Revisited

I have never been so happy to set my eyes on my old friend. Will and wee Robbie had Munro ready for our trip to the new Glenammon Brewery with Duncan.

"I have missed ye so," I said as I kissed the nose of my dear friend that I have not seen enough of since returning to Skye. "Munro, do ye ken I almost told my own husband once that ye were the one I loved most in my life."

"Aye, she did Munro, and I will never forgive ye fer it!" Will said loudly, with a smile of his own back to me. Munro bowed his head to me and ignored Will. My darling lad knows where my loyalties truly lie.

I leaned forward to stroke his neck once I was mounted. I truly loved and missed my Munro. We rode out of the castle gates with Duncan to a portion of the MacLeod lands along the coast between Castle Dunmara and Dunmara Village. It was a short ride, but easier by horse. The newly painted, and impressive stone building did not have the large letters spelling *Glenammon* on the sides but much like its twin on the banks of the Firth of Forth, it was an impressive sight and seemed to be just as bustling. There were many people working on construction of the building and unloading carts of stone, wooden casks, peat, and barley.

"The first thing to ken," Duncan said as we tied up the horses in the front of the building, "is that it is early days. We will have a complex operation much like Leith where we have storage for the ale produced there, along with imported wine for distribution to the Isles, Highlands, and Glasgow. Glenammon Brewing's ledgers showed me that there is as much money to be made on being a storehouse and shipping center as a brewery—if not more."

"I can imagine having such an operation on the western side of the country could be a benefit. It must cost less to send ale and eventually whisky from here to Glasgow, the Highlands, or the Isles, instead of all the way from Edinburgh."

"Exactly, and fer now, it frees up distribution on Leith as they only have to deliver it here. We handle the final distribution beyond. That business buys us some time until the first batches of ale and whisky are ready here."

"And how will ye fare with delivery?" Will asked.

I chimed in with a smile and asked, "By land or by sea, Duncan?"

"Aye, Edinburgh will ship directly to the port at Dunmara Village. We are looking at having our own ferry from the mainland, but the boats will deliver their stores straight to Skye fer now. It is more secure, and we expect delivery once a month, when the sea and weather cooperate, of course! Then, once we make our own ale and whisky here, the shipment from Leith may no longer be needed. We will split coverage of the country."

He walked us through the area designated for the distillery, the drying of the malt, and the grist mill. He walked us through the separation of the grist for fermenting and his housing of casks.

"Come with me and I will give ye a first taste," he said, "but ye ken it needs more time aging in the casks. It will be mighty *strong*."

"We understand there is a process, Duncan," I said, hoping he would know that we would not judge him harshly on his first batches. I looked at Will and said, "But surely a much more refined process than making *mead*."

Will turned green for a second at the horrible memory and then smiled at me. I just looked at Duncan, who looked confused and said, laughing, "Old story."

Duncan poured the first glasses, and the smell was so strong that my eyes watered. "I taste something else with the smokey peat," I said, trying to place the flavor.

"I cannae tell, but it tastes spicy," Will said in agreement.

"Aye lad! I will never tell the secret, but the smoky peat and spices will give it a new flavor, and both are *warm*."

Animated now and proving that my father gave his brother the greatest gift of his life, he said, "I told ye both that whisky can warm ye from the inside and the flavor helps that, not just the alcohol."

"Aye, uncle," I said, smiling at him and taking pride in his accomplishment.

Will said, "I think it is good and will only get richer and darker as it ages in the casks."

"That is right," Duncan said back to him. "The taste will settle down and become smooth as well. Like I said, it is a tad strong just now and tastes unfinished, but ye can see where we are going."

"I am so proud of ye, Duncan!"

Will shook his hand and said, "Ye have done well with yer investment, sir! And I cannae imagine how you have done this much in such a short amount of time."

"I thank ye both! The money I got for the investment and for selling a portion of my stake in the brewery meant I could hire more people to work on the construction of the building, but I also hired Auld Finn Ewan in Fort William, who has been making small batches of whisky for over thirty years to help me with the formulation and the process. Do ye ken, the man?"

We both shook our heads and said together, "No."

"He is not here this day, or I would introduce ye, but the man has a small private operation of his own lands. He supplies most of the whisky to Dunmara Castle to supplement what we make ourselves. He also sells privately to some of the taverns between here and Fort William. I have learned a lot from him over the last few weeks and months. He kens everything about whisky and, at even risk to his own business, has been more than generous with me."

"That is wonderful, Duncan. I suspect we will be one of your first clients when you are ready."

"I am counting on it, my lady," he said with a wink. "Orders from Dunmara Castle would keep us in business on its own."

"Aye! I hear that Clan MacLeod likes their whisky," I said, laughing at him. I suspect Duncan and Angus alone will keep demand high from both Dunmara Castle and the Old Stone Tavern.

"Come with me to the back office," Duncan said, "I have some bottle samples to look at and I welcome yer advice on those as well."

We walked through the large room where they were lining up casks for the ale on one end and to the back door leading to the still housed in a smaller room behind. Duncan had many men working on the project, and it allowed them to make considerable progress. Now they just need to start making the whisky at the same speed as the ale so it could age.

Once we were in the back office, the table was scattered with drawings of the building and ledgers detailing his inventory and expenses. He took us to a long table by the window where there were five bottles lined up. The light from the window facing the sea made each of them sparkle. I knew which one I liked right away, but waited for Will to say something first.

Duncan said, "We might be getting ahead of ourselves, considering I have no whisky yet, but these are the five samples from a glassmaker outside of Glasgow. I have my favorite, but I want to hear what ye think first." I smiled as I thought that this is a new form of the *'what do we think about'* game.

Will and I walked up and held each bottle to inspect in the light of the window behind us. Four of the five were dark glass. The bottles range from a very basic jug with a small circle handle to a thin tall bottle with a large round cork with a *'G'* burned into it. One was clear glass with the same cork.

"I like the tall one with the cork, but I guess it depends how much ye want to manufacture and ship. Some shipments may be better with the large bottles," Will said.

"Aye, lad! It is a fair point. I should have said it at the start—we will mostly sell to our clan and potentially the Old Stone. Most orders will just be in casks. Many of the bottles will be for specific use, provided for Dunmara Castle to fill and deliver to the table to pour. Whisky will not be shipped in bottles. What do ye think, Alex?"

I smiled and said as I picked up the only bottle that was not like the others, "I like this one."

The bottle was well designed. It was clear glass and had the full name *'Glenammon'* etched on the front. It had a similar round cork with the *'G'* as the bottle Will selected.

Duncan smiled and said, *"I kent it!* I told Auld Finn ye would pick this one! Tell us why, lass."

His eyes showed that he was eager for my opinion, as I said, "Well first I like that the glass is clear, because ye will be able to see the golden whisky in it, instead of hiding it behind dark glass. Second, with the etching, it will stand out in every tavern or home as ours. I have never seen one that looks like this! The other bottles I have seen in taverns all look the same and ye often dinnae ken an ale jug from a whisky jug on a table. In fact, I think there is usually only one type of jug fer both."

William and Duncan both smiled and nodded their heads as I made my case. Duncan said, "Yer cross-country tour of Scottish taverns has paid off then, lass! The distribution beyond our clan lands could put us in the sights of the tax man. This is why all the jugs looks the same. Often barkeeps hide whisky, if they have it at all, in the same jugs that ale is in."

"I didna ken that," I said. "we have been so open about finding whisky on our travels."

"Aye, it has been an open secret. More so on Skye and the Highlands. The tax man is not all that inclined to venture to the remote portions of Scotland."

"Because they dinnae often return to England, if they do," Will said openly. Duncan nodded that this was indeed the truth.

I just looked at them both and asked, "Then Jacob took a risk having whisky fer us at the White Hart?"

"Perhaps, but Jacob is an honest man. My guess is that he kens what he was up against and bought from a small reputable maker like Sir Alexander does and the cost paid likely covered the tax. Also, I suspect the whisky in his cellar sits in a cask marked as ale. It is no wonder whisky is often delivered in the same brown jug or an ale pot in some taverns."

I smiled thinking of Jacob taking a risk for his friends and said, "Then I will tell ye as family, I am sure it costs money, but I like the etching of the name on the bottle. We are not yet there, but I fully expect that if we want to get the name out there where people eventually *ask* for our whisky, they should see that it is, in fact, *Glenammon*. Come to think of it, the same could be said for our ale. Dark jug or not, it *should* have our name on it! Not just the cask in the cellar! The man with coin in his pocket asking for Glenammon should feel when it arrives as his table that it is indeed what he asked fer."

I handed the bottle back to my uncle, now suddenly quiet as my mind raced. All the thoughts about the brewery and potential of the distillery made me think of my father and of the future. If we learned anything during our time in Edinburgh, and the clues he left us all, my father was ahead of his time. He perhaps understood the future more than most. And I am Alexander MacLeod's daughter, after all!

Duncan looked at me and asked, "Ye have more to say?" I smiled at him, because I did have more to say, and I appreciated he knew me well enough to see my thinking in the moment.

"Ye can always read my mind!"

"No! I can read yer face! It gives me the clues to yer mind clear enough," Duncan said, as he and Will laughed together. My face has betrayed my thinking once again and these men do, in fact, know how to read it. I nodded to each of them in resignation of this fact.

"Duncan, I ken that ye have thought of creating another brewery on this side of the country to benefit the future of the distillery, which can be three years or more out of producing anything."

"That is right, lass! I kent that I could not have a leadership role at Glenammon living here on the other side of the country, and kent that a warehouse on the western side of Scotland could save even more than just on the cost of transportation and distribution. It is a good first start to store from Leith, but a functioning brewery here can reduce shipping costs and increase profits even more. The distillery is a future endeavor that is not accounted for in Leith. The small share I sold to Drummond buys us this building and the initial development of what is needed fer us to have both a brewery *and* distillery on Skye."

I stepped away from them and looked out the window to the bay and then back at the grand operation Duncan was building as my mind raced with even more ideas. These men could see my mind working and waited for me to speak again.

"What are ye thinking, lass?" Duncan finally asked as he looked at both me and Will.

"I want us to talk to Campbell."

"Campbell?" Will asked.

"Aye," I said, correcting myself and my informality and suddenly realizing the heart of his question. "I apologize. I want us to talk to Master Forbes."

"What can our advocate do fer us?" Duncan asked. Will looked at me likely thinking the same.

"This entire building is yers sir, and I told ye owe me no accounting of yer operations here. I think ye have a solid plan."

"But?"

"I mean no offense, but I have an idea, if ye will permit me."

"I take no offense with yer ideas. That is why I invited ye and Will here in such early stages. Please! I value yer opinion! What are ye thinkin'?"

I smiled at him and said, "What if we buy Master Drummond out and keep *all* of Glenammon Brewing *and* the future Glenammon Distillery in MacLeod hands? East and West. *All of Scotland.*"

Will and Duncan were shocked at my words and looked at each other as I continued, "Alexander MacLeod built this! He built the name Glenammon! And I want us—his family and Clan MacLeod—to *reclaim* it!"

They both nodded but were still trying to follow my thinking. "Think about it! We have started thinking about new ways to make income on our lands, aye? First, we started with sheep. That enterprise, while good, is starting to become unmanageable with people vacating the clan lands.

We already ken there is some economy of scale having operations on both sides of the country for distribution. Done. Then ye add the brewing of ale—again on both sides of the country—and the possibilities could be endless. Glasgow and Edinburgh are port cities with direct routes to England, and then Edinburgh to France and broader Europe, and Glasgow to Ireland and beyond."

I became more animated at the thought of building Glenammon to be even more than it is. "Then, sir! With the scale of such operations, we can add the distillery of whisky on Skye. But thinking about the future, I can see us offering positions fer work on Skye outside of the traditional fishing, farming, and shepherding fer those that want to remain here. And Duncan!! Think of it! Fer those that believe they *must* go to the cities fer another life, we can try to keep them employed at our own operations there in distribution."

Will spoke up and added to my thinking, "If yer operations grow, ye could even have people in the colonies and beyond."

"That is right, Will," I said to him, placing my hand on his arm and the other on my head, "MacLeod kinsman serving MacLeod interests along with their own. It will take some time, perhaps many years, but believe we can do this, sir!"

Duncan came to me and hugged me and kissed me on the forehead. Smiling at me, he said, "My darlin' lass! Erm, my lady!! My brothers and I kent ye would be a fine chief and every day ye prove that we were right. Ye seem to understand the business of drink even more than even I could."

Will smiled at me proudly and I said to Duncan, "Then, if ye agree, I will send a message to Master Forbes and ask him to come see us. Ye can give him yer tour and he can tell us if this idea can work. He can also give us the counsel we need to help make it so and negotiate with Master Drummond on our behalf to buy him out fully."

I took a moment and said, "I would also verra much like to see Elizabeth," I said relaxing my shoulders and thinking of my dear friend with a smile. "Are we all agreed?"

"Aye," both men said to me with confidence.

"If we can work out the timing, I think it would be good for Master Forbes to see the summer operations on our lands. He is our advocate, after all."

Duncan said, "Aye, it will be good learning fer him to see what we do here across *all* of our lands, and that includes the shearing."

+++

I sent my letters to Master Forbes and to my dear friend Elizabeth. I celebrated their marriage and asked them to please come to us on Skye. We need their support! And the timing with the summer lads could not be more perfect for our advocate to visit Dunmara.

They both sent lovely letters in response, each eagerly agreeing to visit us. I worked with Knox, Duncan, and Missus Gerrard on our plan to welcome and celebrate them as our special guests at Castle Dunmara for one week in late July. They would have the best accommodations and we would have a feast and cèilidh in their honor.

I have never been so happy to have a diversion and special guests, our friends, here on Skye and show them a different way of life from the busy and crowded city. This was also my first chance as Lady MacLeod to host guests at Dunmara.

Will joined me in my chamber and stood behind my chair, rubbing my shoulders. I shared each of the letters with him.

"Ye will be verra happy to have her here," Will said in my ear from behind me.

"Aye," I said, grabbing his hand and kissing it as the other wrapped around me, "I have no women in my life that are not *mothers*, and she has been a good friend to me. *Och my!* How she saw exactly what you were doing at my birthday supper!"

Will pulled back slightly, asking, "And what was that?"

"Ye wanted my attention," I said sweetly and kissing his hand again.

He hugged me tight and said, "That I did, but *mostly* I wanted ye to agree with me."

I stood and kissed him on the mouth before saying, "She said the same, but I would never give in to yer argument!" Will kissed me on my forehead, accepting my words as truth. The man knew that I would never give in.

"She has never said anything to me, but I ken she loved my father and I believe he loved her because Will, I *love* her. I ken that there is a reason she is in my life. I love her!"

"Aye! Let us go to supper and we can talk more about yer plans for their visit and how I can be of help to ye."

SEVEN
Truth And Lies

Dunmara Castle
Isle of Skye, Scotland
May 1767

I walked into the classroom and found Master Harmon picking up parchment and closing ink wells on desks. He immediately walked to me as I entered the room and seemed somewhat surprised to see me here.

"Sir, I wanted to see how things are progressing with the larger classes."

I find it interesting again that I try to speak the King's English when talking to Master Harmon. I temper my Scottish accent and speak in a much more formal manner than I do each day. It sounds so ridiculous coming out of my mouth, but I continue to do it, anyway.

"Lady MacLeod, it has gone quite well! With the girls starting from the same point, it has been easier to manage the class. I only have one young man who can read, and Robbie, as you know, is just a step behind, but knows his letters and can write his name. Most are on the same level here, starting with the basics. That makes it easy to plan the day in a way that helps them all progress together."

"And how are the lasses faring, sir?"

"They are all doing quite well and are most eager to learn. I have also been pleasantly surprised at how they help each other so willingly throughout the day. It is a joy to watch! They want to learn!"

I smiled at the thought that our experiment could work, but chose not to broach the subject of the possibility of educating all children throughout our lands, and not just at the surrounding castle. That was more than we could both imagine, and to take children away from family would be a challenge. That is, until I thought about how during summer, when we have so many here, we might work in education with shearing and apprenticeships. Once again, my mind started thinking ahead of itself.

"I also want to know how Master Robbie is performing in yer class.

"The boy is short on confidence due to his injury, but he is more than capable."

"I agree," I said and paused, as it seemed he had more to say. "And?"

"I think the boy may need spectacles. I am not an expert on this, but I believe his left eye could use some support as it overcompensates for the right. It is noticeable when he writes his letters. He squints his eyes tight during the task. I think it will be become even more pronounced when he tries to read. Not having the support of the glass spectacles, he could strain his good eye and suffer headaches because of it."

"Och, of course!"

He read the worry on my face and said, "The young man will be fine! I meant no offense to Master Robbie."

"No offense taken, sir! I just want him to be successful. The lad is important to our family."

He placed his hand on my arm and said, "Spectacles will only help the boy and make his studies and advancement easier."

I smiled at him in understanding and then I realized that the man was closer to me than he should be. We just looked at each other and then he leaned in to kiss me softly on the lips.

Will was the only man I have ever kissed, and while Harmon's kiss did not have the same passion, it was tender. It was not aggressive like Wesley's and landed on my lips sweetly. I stepped back and said, staring at the floor, unable to look at him in the eye, "That must *never* happen again, sir."

This was not acceptable in any way, and it was my own weakness that allowed Master Harmon to kiss me. I could have turned my head and stopped him like I did with Wesley, but for some reason I did not. I am not completely certain if I was not expecting it or if I wanted to it. Either way, I felt ashamed for my part in it.

I had to tell Will the truth of it and try my best to keep my jealous husband from killing the only educator we have on the MacLeod clan lands.

+++

After supper, I joined Will in our chamber. I got ready for bed and waited for Will. We both had our books of sonnets open to read. Sometimes we read together and sometimes we read on our own. I have Lady Margaret's book and Will's gift from my birthday. Sometimes Will reads from my father's book secured at MacLeod House. There is no shortage of sonnets in this bedchamber. We read together in silence this night.

He kissed me after we put our books down and before we extinguished the candles and I said in a whisper, "Will, I have something to say to ye."

"Aye, love," he said softly anticipating my words.

I just looked at him for a moment and he tilted his head to me, uncertain now of what I might say after such a long pause. I was searching for my words but had to just say the truth of it. I owed him that. I owed him nothing but the truth.

"Master Harmon kissed me today."

In an instant, my loving husband raised himself from our bed and marched toward the fire in a raging anger. I expected it, but it shocked me all the same. He is not a small man, so his reaction was intense and powerful!

"Please, sir," I begged running after him, "it was innocent!"

"How is kissing another man's wife *innocent? Christ above!*"

"Will," I said, standing next to him now and touching his cheek. "Calm yerself and listen to me, *please!*"

He was enraged and said nothing, but his eyes showed me he was as hurt as he was angry.

"*Innocent?*"

"*Please*. Listen to me. I am telling ye the *truth* of it."

"Och, lass! Tell me *all* about the *truth* of it!'

"Will..."

"I encourage ye to read Sonnet one hundred and thirty-eight when ye have a chance. No! No! Let me do that fer ye this verra moment!"

Will stared at me as I tried to remember the content of the verse and how it could possibly relate to this conversation. Before I could, he opened his book and started to read it aloud, landing on every blistering word with the anger he felt at me in this moment.

> **"When my love swears that she is made of truth,**
> **I do believe her though I know she lies,**
> That she might think me some untutored youth,
> Unlearned in the world's false subtleties.
> Thus vainly thinking that she thinks me young,
> Although she knows my days are past the best,
> **Simply I credit her false-speaking tongue:**
> **On both sides thus is simple truth suppressed:**
> But wherefore says she not she is unjust?
> And wherefore say not I that I am old?
> O! love's best habit is in seeming trust,
> And age in love, loves not to have years told:
> > Therefore I lie with her, and she with me,
> **And in our faults by lies we flattered be."**
> > **Sonnet 138,** William Shakespeare

"That isna fair!" I said in pain at the words he chose and the manner in which he said them. The meaning of the verse did not fully fit, but his meaning was clear enough in his reading of the first two lines. Will believes me a liar. That was his only message to me with this selection.

"I cannae believe ye let that man touch ye," Will said as he hung his head in shame and disgust. Then he looked at me in the eye and said, "But what should I *expect* when ye are in the school with him every day?"

"He didna touch me!"

I corrected myself when he looked at me in disbelief, "I mean, I didna *let* him touch me! I have *never lied* to ye, Will."

"Aye," he said to me, angrier than I have ever seen him as he stepped to me with tears in his eyes.

"Ye *never lied* to me about cutting yer body!"

I stepped back from him again as he continued his litany of accusations.

"Ye *never lied* to me about not eating!"

I stepped back again until I was stopped by the mantle in front of the fire.

"Ye *never lied* to me about Calder touching ye!"

"Will, I didna lie!" I said in a whisper as the last broke my heart and my tears started to fall.

I was so hurt that he brought up Calder that just added to the feeling that I would never escape his ghost and the pain of knowing that my own husband did not understand that the man was the primary source of my pain and anguish since we left Edinburgh. All the acts of harm I have committed on my own body and the torment I felt in my mind and my soul since the day the intruder came into our home, his words hurt me almost more than anything else.

I yelled through my tears, "I *never lied* to ye!"

"Ye did not *tell the truth*, woman," he said coldly and turned his back to me. *"Is there a difference?"*

I could not breathe. His words sucked the air out of my lungs. I have never seen Will so angry, and it hurt me to feel his anger directed toward me. I knew most of his resentment was out of his own wounded male pride and jealousy. But he was right. There is no difference.

Is not telling the truth the same as a lie?

When does a secret become a lie?

When do the sins of omission seed half-truths and distrust between people that love each other?

There is no difference.

But I could not keep my mouth shut. If Will was going to hurt me, I was going to hurt him right back. It was a moment of immaturity, but the mention of Calder was more than I could bear this night.

"I just *tried* to tell ye the truth of it, out of respect to ye as my husband! And ye with all yer willful and *foolish* male pride willna listen to me because ye are too busy measuring cocks with someone that is *no threat* to ye!"

He did not move, and I hit him on his back, forcing him to turn around and look at me. I said in pain, almost unable to breathe when he finally did, "I have suffered so because of what Calder did to me and... my own husband *cannae* see it! Ye ken what he did to my body, and what he does to me still in my head, and ye said the words to hurt me, anyway! *How could ye?*"

His eyes showed me that he regretted his words. But I did not stop my own barrage of resentment and anger. In fact, his silence only incensed me more!

"I *hate* ye fer that! I will *hate ye forever* fer it!"

Now Will was backing away from me as I unleashed every negative thought I ever had on him.

"I *hate* ye fer leaving me alone so that man could rape me and kill my child, setting me on a course of constant misery! I am haunted *every* day by Calder and ye simply choose to ignore it! I told myself for years I would never marry, and I should have *never* married ye, *William Lachlan MacCrimmon!*"

I remembered he told me how he likes to hear me say his full name and I just destroyed that forever as I spat out each of his names with total venom. I could see instantly that he was hurt by what I said and came back at me with a fury and stopped himself just before me, nostrils flaring and red-faced. He did so because he loves me, but I was already determined to hurt him as much as he hurt me... and *I was not finished.*

I looked down as I saw his fist forming and said with all the rage I had left, "Aye, do it! *Do it! Ye are yer father's son.*"

I said the horrible words as both a command and a wish. I could not blame him for reacting to my litany of hurtful words, but I hated myself at that very moment. I did not realize until now how much Will was still another point of pain for me. My husband was another ghost haunting me at times.

I regretted the words I said immediately as Will backed away from me, clearly wounded. His face told me I had hurt him more so than telling him Master Harmon kissed me. I should have *never* said what I did!

I could not find the words to recover from such a horrible thing. He is not his father, and I am not his mother.

He would *never* hit me, but I made it sound like it was possible. I made it sound like I *wanted* him to. My words shattered us both.

I tried to correct myself, and said in a whisper as I reached for him, "*Will...*"

With tears in his eyes, he walked out of the room without saying another word to me. He did not return. After crying before the fire, I walked down to the hall and the kitchen to see if he was there so that I could try to make this right and correct myself.

I decided that if he were in the stables, that would not be the place to continue this discussion and returned to my room where I finally fell asleep in tears for my husband's pain and my own regret for the hateful words I said to him in anger.

+++

At breakfast the next morning, Duncan asked across the empty seat between us.

"Where is Will this morn'?"

I just looked at him with tears in my eyes.

"Stop, lass. We will talk in yer chamber," he said, looking about the room, hoping no one else saw my moment of weakness at the head table. I shook and cried with the misery of what had happened the night before, and he ushered me out of the room.

When we arrived at my chamber, I fell into his arms and sobbed. When I could catch my breath, I said through my tears, "I was *horrible* to him! We had a fight about Master Harmon kissing me and, after everything that was said, he accused me of being a liar..."

"He did *what?*" Duncan said. "Not Will! Harmon!"

"*Uncle*," I said quietly and with a shameful look of embarrassment.

"Och, *Alex*," he said as he lowered his head, clearly disappointed in me, as much if not more than Harmon.

"It was unfortunate. I told the man that it cannae happen again. I came to my husband with the truth of it *that verra night*, and that was not enough fer Will and his jealous nature!"

My uncle handed me his handkerchief, as he always does as I continued, "He accused me of spending too much time with Master Harmon at the school and seemed to be of the thinking that I must have behaved in an improper way for it to have happened. Then we started yelling at each other. He accused me of being a liar!"

Duncan said nothing, and I caught my breath again and continued, "Will accused me of lying about cutting myself and not eating, but then he said that I lied about Calder touching me. I was so hurt by him bringing up Calder—who ye ken *haunts* me *every day*—that I tried to hurt him as much as he hurt me. So, I accused Will of leaving me alone and that his error resulted in Calder raping and beating me."

"Och, lass," he said, bowing his head again, knowing that I was still carrying the resentment of Will for what happened at Canongate. He thought that he had helped mend this thinking in my bedchamber in Edinburgh, but here we were again. He was likely also carrying his own guilt for leaving me alone. I could see the pain he felt in his eyes that I blamed one man for that terrible day.

"That is not the worst of it!"

Duncan looked at me, confused about what could possibly be worse than telling your husband that his absence led to your brutal rape and the death of his child.

"I told him I *hated* him and that I *wished* that I had never married him. He was so hurt by my words and the way I said them, he charged at me. I ken because he had tears in his eyes. He *was hurt*. I hurt him. I hurt him on purpose. And then I said... then I said... *that he was like his father.*"

I had told Duncan about Will's history with his father beating his mother and he shut his eyes and sighed and said, *"Ye didna."*

"Aye, I did," I said through my sorrowful tears and shame. "I regretted it the minute the words came out of my mouth. *But I couldna take them back.* I ken he was hurt and angry, but he would never hit me. I have no idea where Will is. He left me at once and did not return in the night."

Duncan hugged me as I cried through my regret and then pushed me forward to look at me in the eyes and said, "The lad is in the stables."

I looked at him and sighed with relief and he continued, "I saw the man there this morning, but didna speak to him. I thought I would just see him at the head table."

"I ken I was wrong, and I would never want to hurt Will, but what I said must have been festering underneath for me to say such horrible things to him. How do I correct myself?"

Duncan just looked at me and shook his head. He had no advice for me just yet.

"Uncle! I told my own husband that I *hated* him," I said again as I bowed my head in shame and in tears, "more than once and I dinnae ken how ye come back from that! The words have not only been said, but *they have been heard!* Tell me how to mend it! I dinnae ken what to do! I love him! *I dinnae ken what to do!*"

Before Duncan could give me his advice, wee Robbie came running into the chamber door and said, "My lady, ye need to come down to the Great Hall. *Now!*"

We followed Robbie frantically down the stairs to find Will laid out on a table. I ran for him and asked, "What happened? Is he alive?"

Robbie said, "He was kicked by Thunder into the wood fence of the paddock. We think he is just out cold, but Auld Knox has gone to collect Master Morrison to help."

I put my hands around Will's calm and peaceful face, the boyish face I see when he sleeps, and a face much different from the one I saw the night before. I could see he was bleeding from his head, but I could tell he was alive. I could feel the warmth of his face and I could feel his breath on my hands. I placed the handkerchief Duncan offered me before on the wound at the side of Will's head.

"My darlin' man, ye will be just fine. Ye will be just fine! Hold on, my love!"

Master Morrison arrived and evaluated his injuries. He said the kick landed on his right shoulder and arm and would likely be bruised and sore. You could clearly see the mark that was red and swollen. He did not think anything was broken or that the shoulder was out of joint. He put his arm in a sling tight to his chest to keep it still, just in case, until he could talk to the man. He said the head wound would resolve itself with care and told me what to do as I helped him clean and wrap it. I was to do the same the next day with a clean cloth.

Master Morrison did not see anything that caused him great concern other than the fact that the man was still not awake. He said that we would have to observe Will carefully over the next few hours and that he would come back to check on him. I had the men who brought him inside carry Will up to our bedchamber. Missus Gerrard saw to our every need for water, broth, and food, as she and a very worried Master Knox checked on us throughout the night.

Master Morrison came to see us again later that evening and did seem concerned that Will was still not responsive, but tried his best not to worry me. I did not sleep and in the early hours of the morning when Will was still not awake, I started to become concerned myself. I kept talking to him and putting my head constantly on his chest to ensure he was still breathing. He was, and it gave me some comfort. I just needed him to wake.

At some point, I said to him in tears over his chest and holding his hand, "William Lachlan MacCrimmon, I *promise* ye, I will never ever speak to ye the way I did last night. I *promise* ye! What I said, I did out of my own pain and anger and ye didna deserve it."

I held my husband and ran my fingers through his curls, whispering over and over in his ear as I cried, "*I am so sorry, Will. I am so verra sorry. I am afraid that if ye leave me, I will live in regret fer the rest of my life that last ye have of me was that horrible moment... my anger and hateful words.*"

Suddenly, I could feel his hands in my hair. I sat up immediately and began kissing him all over his face.

"Och, Will! I am so verra sorry for everything I said."

"Aye, I heard," he said with a smile, and took my chin. "I figured if I kept my eyes closed long enough, ye would eventually apologize to me."

"I should strike ye in that sore shoulder for your deceit, man! Ye gave me fits of worry not waking," I said with a laugh through my tears. His attempt at humor after the awful things we said to each other showed me he had the same regret I did.

"No. I should have *never* said what I did to ye, love. And I should *never* come at ye with such raw anger."

"*Will*," I whispered as I kissed him fully on his mouth. *"Never again! Never again* will we leave each other in anger like we did last night! We will have many disagreements in our lifetime together, but whatever the argument, we can step away to collect ourselves if we need to. But we cannot leave each other in this life with such hateful words. We have to make it right with each other."

He took my hair and brought me to him for another kiss and said, "I agree. *Never again.*"

I pulled back from him and asked, "How do ye feel, my love?"

"I feel like I have been kicked by a horse," he said with a smile as he touched his shoulder and then his head with his free hand.

I laughed at his humor again and said, "Aye, and ye landed in the paddock fence. Yer chest and shoulder took the kick, and Master Morrison put ye in a sling to keep yer arm stable until he could talk to ye. Ye have a large bump and cut on yer head, and we will have to change the cloth every day, but the healer was of the mind that ye will be fine. We were just worried that ye were not waking fer so long. Do ye want me to send fer him?"

"No, I just want ye here with me."

After a while, holding on to each other, I said, "I have been trying to recover from Edinburgh fer some time, but we are still struggling. I am still struggling."

"Aye, look at me," he said as I sat up to look at him across his chest. He touched my face and said, "I think that every man sees what I do. Ye are beautiful, smart, and kind." I smiled at the compliment, and sighed, all the while knowing that I did not demonstrate these positive traits in any way during our last conversation. "And I believe that if every man can see what I do that they will also want to bed ye."

I pulled away for a moment at his words, "I mean no offense other than to say, I trust *no man* with ye. I ken now that I held ye accountable fer my jealousy of Master Harmon—and Master Forbes before him. My words and my jealous nature were telling ye that I didna trust *ye*. I *do* trust ye as my wife, love. *I do.*"

"Will, if ye havena noticed, I am surrounded by men. With the exception of Missus Gerrard in the management of this house, men lead every other aspect of our clan lands and the running of the castle. Men that I will have to deal with constantly as Lady MacLeod. I fear that if ye are jealous of all of these men, then ye will be miserable in yer marriage to me. I dinnae have a choice because of my responsibility, but I dinnae want ye to be constant misery fer it."

"Aye, ye told me all of this before we married, but I have not been good at remembering yer words. Ye should not be burdened by my male pride and jealousy."

We were silent for a moment when he finally continued. "I *was* jealous of the time ye were spending with Master Harmon. I was angered that he kissed ye, but I should have respected that ye told me the truth of it right away and I didna. I am verra sorry for that. All I could feel in the moment was my anger at the man and I took that anger out on ye. I was wrong."

Looking down at our hands holding on to each other, he continued, "I dinnae want to be miserable, but if I am honest, I was also jealous that both men that have caused me the most worry are more educated."

I took his face in my hands and said, my tears flowing at his words, "Stop this thinking *now*! *Yer my man!* In the stables, or in the forge, or in the fields—yer *here with me now*! Yer my man *forever*! We promised each other *forever*, did we not?"

"Aye, we did."

After sitting quietly for a moment, I said softly, "Will, what I said about ye being yer father's son, I am *so* ashamed. *It was hateful... and it was unfair!* I cannae take the words back, but I am *so verra* sorry."

"Think nothing of it again. We both hurt each other with our words and we both ken better."

"No. It pains me so because it was not just that I said the words, but I said them *on purpose* to hurt ye. I kent what I was doing, and that only adds to my shame and regret! I ken ye would never hit me, love! I do! *Please forgive me!*"

"Forgiven."

I kissed his mouth and said, "If we are honest with each other like this night, I believe we can conquer anything. But we have to respect each other. I owe ye that as my husband and my *friend*."

"Aye, I owe ye the same, my darlin' wife... and *friend*."

+++

EIGHT
The Loss Of The Laird

Dunmara Castle
Isle of Skye, Scotland
May 1767

Laird Graham's bedchamber reflected his love of the land and sea surrounding the castle, and he had the artwork and books to prove it. Watercolor paintings and ink sketches of the castle grounds, the sea cliffs, and the details on the landscapes and wildlife native to our island home fill the room. Since Lady Margaret's death, he has been prolific in his work here in his bedchamber and the laird's chamber.

Pointing to the ledgers at the end of the table next to his bed, Laird Graham said, "Alexandra, ye will find the records of the last gatherings in the Great Hall since ye left and the financial ledgers here. All is good fer Clan MacLeod. After the summer lads left, we sold a great deal of wool and finished cloth. The fishing hauls remained strong, so much so that we could fill our stores and have fine meals. We made sales in the village and even as far as Glasgow. We even had a good sale to Fort William."

"Keeping us in good stead with the Crown, no doubt."

"Aye," he said with a wink, "yer always thinking like a clan chief!"

"But as predicted, more tenants are starting to leave us for the cities and the colonies. Ye will want to look at the map with Master Knox and think about the plan before the next round of summer lads arrives. And ye ken we have added more sheep, both from purchases and a strong lambing season. I fear that the numbers this year will impact the assignments in a new way."

"I understand, sir."

"The challenge will be that we may not have the lads in number to help across the lands and the shearing. Ye may even have to involve the lasses in the shearing and not just in the treatment of the wool."

As much as I needed to catch up on the running of the clan lands, I really just wanted to be with him in this moment. So much of our life has changed since I left for Edinburgh, and his health has steadily become worse since our return.

He knows what I have had to endure, and he knows I have struggled personally with the painful memories that haunt me. He needs to feel confident in his choice of me as successor and while I am still trying to find myself on some days, I am stronger than I have allowed myself to be as of late. I also just want to be with him, talk with him, and learn from him... while I have him.

"May I sit and read with ye, a while, my laird?"

"Aye, lass, the sonnets are just there," he said as he pointed to the book on his bedside table.

"Father Bruce is on his way soon. But we have some time together, my dear."

I opened the book, began reading where he had left off and said, "It is Sonnet Thirty, sir."

I knew this sonnet and looked at him again, knowing that the content may be more poignant than expected for a man who is unwell. He seemed he also knew it but nodded to me to read it, anyway.

"When to the sessions of sweet silent thought
I summon up remembrance of things past,
I sigh the lack of many a thing I sought,
And with old woes new wail my dear time's waste:
Then can I drown an eye, unused to flow,
For precious friends hid in death's dateless night,
And weep afresh love's long since cancell'd woe,
And moan the expense of many a vanish'd sight:
Then can I grieve at grievances foregone,
And heavily from woe to woe tell o'er
The sad account of fore-bemoaned moan,
Which I new pay as if not paid before.
    But if the while I think on thee, dear friend,
    All losses are restor'd and sorrows end."

Sonnet 30, William Shakespeare

"Aye, that is a beloved sonnet, lass. And one that rings true to an old man on his deathbed."

"It rings true to me, as well," I said, closing the book looking out toward the light of the window on the other side of the room. I ran my fingers over the scars on my left arm. "We waste so much time in our own self-imposed suffering."

"Aye, lass. That we do. *That we do.* We surround ourselves with insecurities and doubt. Incessant worry over things we cannae change. And we shield our hearts in this fear and doubt, afraid to let others get close to us."

I smiled, thinking about Lady Margaret, my own attempts at protecting my heart upon his words. I then thought of my beloved Will.

"Or even help us, sir." He nodded and let me continue, as I said softly as I smiled at him in silent understanding, "We also find ways to hurt ourselves before someone else can."

I could see he was listening to me intently, and perhaps allowing me to continue my most recent confessions. He had already heard these words from me from our conversation at my bedside. But the sonnet brought it all back to me. I tried to shift our talk to more of a positive tone. "But that is the gift of Master Shakespeare, is it not? Reminding us of all of our human frailties?"

He did not let me brush past the sonnet's meaning so quickly.

"Now that you are married to William, ye must not have such laments, dear Alexandra."

"Is that so, my laird?" I said as I smiled at him in appreciation of his thoughts on marriage and a woman's mind.

"The man loves ye, lass. It is clear to all that see him look at ye when ye walk into a room, or speak, or laugh."

"Duncan said the same thing," I said, smiling. I could feel the color rise in my cheeks at this statement. I love William and I know that he loves me. But, to hear my uncle say that he can *see* that love, tells me all I needed to know—all I needed reminding of. William will be my love and my life forever. I am so blessed to know that his love will help wash away my worries and laments. His love will save me from others and maybe save me from myself. I just have to give him the chance to do so.

"He is a good husband to me."

"He is indeed! Trust him, lass. He will be a valued partner fer ye in many ways. Just as Lady Margaret was to me, y'ken?"

I nodded in agreement and gripped his hand in shared remembrance of Lady Margaret. "Aye, she was a devoted partner, sir!"

"We should all be so lucky to have someone who loves us for all that we are *and* makes us better at the same time."

Somehow, I knew that his words were not just about Will. He was talking about *all* that surround us. He was talking about Duncan, Angus, Robbie, Missus Gerrard, and Auld Knox... all who love us and want us to be successful. I realized in that moment and smiled that I had so much love around me that I smiled widely at the realization as Duncan's words came back to me about not realizing I was surrounded by good company and love.

He looked at me with misty eyes and said in a weary voice, "Ye should go now, Alexandra. I must rest."

I placed his book of sonnets on the table by his bed. I kissed him on the cheek and grabbed his hand as I said, "Rest well, sir. We will continue with the Sonnet Thirty-one tomorrow, aye?"

He looked at me and I looked at him. We both smiled and held our stare for what seemed like an eternity. I walked out of the room and stood against the stone wall in the hall before his chamber in tears.

We both knew that Sonnet Thirty was the last we would read together.

+++

Laird Graham died peacefully in his sleep overnight. Duncan came for me, just as he had for Lady Margaret, but this time there was no urgency for the final goodbye. We stood together as a family around his bed—Duncan, Will, and myself—as Father Bruce led us in prayer.

I regretted that I did not tell him more about how much he meant to me, but I have to believe he knew my heart as much as I knew his.

Father Bruce kissed me on the cheek as he said, "My lady."

"Thank ye Father Bruce. I leave the decisions to Duncan as the last of the brothers and will assist ye both however ye need."

Duncan spoke and said, "It is all pretty standard but, ye can help Missus Gerrard guide the feast and... celebration of life, my lady."

"Aye, sir! I am at yer service."

Over the next several days, Father Bruce guided us through the funeral planning. Laird Graham will be reunited with his beloved wife in the crypt in St. Margaret's chapel, and our family and clan will mourn his loss.

+++

Much like the funeral for Lady Margaret, we kept the burial service to only family, though now that included Will. As sad as I was, there was indeed comfort that he was with his beloved again in spirit.

I held Will's hand as tight as I could, thinking one day we would part in this life, and I could not bear the thought of life without him. His eyes and his comforting smile told me he was likely thinking the same.

We left Duncan in the chapel so that he could say goodbye to his last brother on his own. Much like father's grave, I could not bear to watch him grieve and believe he deserved the privacy to do so on his own.

As we started back to the Castle, I stopped in the courtyard and said, "Will, I will join ye shortly. I need to go to Cairn's Point."

He kissed me and said, "I understand."

And he did. He knew that this was the second father I have lost in a year and that the loss would likely make me think of my parents even more. I did think of my parents today and once I arrived at the cairn, I touched their names, that of wee James Douglas, and even my two carved lines reflecting my lost bairns, before I sat on the ground.

At first, I just breathed in the salty sea air and tried to will the rhythmic peace of the sea below to calm my nerves and emotions. Then I just released all the emotion I had for all that I have lost.

After crying, I tried to think of Will and his positive view. Surely, I had more to celebrate and appreciate what they have given me in life, but sometimes it is hard to see the positive when all you feel is *pain*. The constant struggle has been a trial for me this year, and the huge swings from great happiness and sadness have taken a toll on me.

"Alexandra!"

As he came up the hill, I was so glad to see Duncan, who sat with me on the ground. I smiled at him and took his hand in mine.

"How are ye, sir?"

He shook his head and said, "I dinnae ken. It is hard to lose yer last brother and I feel..." I waited for him to finish his thought before responding, and just held his hand in mine. "I... feel... *alone*."

"Och, Duncan!" I said, now wrapping my arms around him in a loving embrace, trying my best to support him while my heart was breaking with his.

His tears started, and he could barely speak the words, "I am the last brother, and it fills my heart with such grief! To lose Adrian so young, then Alexander, and now Graham. It hurts me. *It hurts me!* We should have all become old men together. Sitting in the Great Hall with gray hair, reliving the stories of our lives and here I am, the last."

"I am so sorry! I am so *verra* sorry."

We sat holding on to each other for a bit in silence. We listened to the sea below and started to watch the sun set below the horizon and tried to heal our wounded hearts.

"Duncan, do ye ken how much I depend on ye?"

"Aye, but lass, ye have to ken that I depend on ye. We are all we have left."

"Then we have to stay here for each other," I said, smiling at him. "I love ye."

"I love ye with all of my heart! Let us get out of the cold now that the sun is down, and I bet yer husband is looking fer ye," he said, kissing my forehead before helping me up off of the cold and damp ground.

+++

This time, Will was leaning on my chest as I wrapped my fingers around his curls and kissed the top of his head. I explained the last meeting with Laird Graham to him and said, "He kent we would never read Sonnet Thirty-one together."

"I am so verra sorry, love," he said, sitting up and looking at me. "Will ye read it to me?"

I sat up and then kissed his mouth for his kindness before taking the book from the bedside table and turning to the page. I sat behind him and brought the book before us on his chest so we could both see the words. I began to read aloud.

> "Thy bosom is endeared with all hearts,
> Which I by lacking have supposed dead;
> And there reigns Love, and all Love's loving parts,
> And all those friends which I thought buried.
> How many a holy and obsequious tear
> Hath dear religious love stol'n from mine eye,
> As interest of the dead, which now appear
> But things removed that hidden in thee lie!
> Thou art the grave where buried love doth live,
> Hung with the trophies of my lovers gone,
> Who all their parts of me to thee did give,
> That due of many now is thine alone:
>> Their images I loved, I view in thee,
>> And thou (all they) hast all the all of me."

Sonnet 31, William Shakespeare

I lost my voice for a moment on the last line as the hot tears ran down my cheeks and said, "I think it is a continuation of Sonnet Thirty. It was his farewell to his loves and to his clan. And *he kent we would never read this one together.*"

+++

NINE
The Lady MacLeod Of MacLeod

In the laird's chamber that has now become mine, Duncan pulled three bottles of claret from a leather bag and placed them on the desk. Will and I looked at him as if he were mad and then he pulled the quaich down from the back shelf and placed it before me.

"Ye have to drink the entire thing," Duncan said. Clarifying his direction, "An entire bottle, at once."

"Thank Christ! I thought I had to drink three bottles. But still, that is not possible! I thought this was just for the men to show their worth or manhood. Do I *really* have to do it as a woman?"

"Lass, every chief of Clan Macleod has to assume the role by drinking an entire bottle of claret out of the quaich before the Great Hall.

We need to practice," he said, as he now brought several small loaves of bread out of his bag.

"This will help," he said, handing each of us our own loaf. "The good news is yer speech is before the drink. And all ye have to really do is say ye agree to take on the responsibility ye have been given. Ye will just answer the question from me before the room on yer commitment, aye?"

"Aye."

"And when finished, lass, Will and I will carry ye out of the room immediately," he said, looking at Will, who nodded in agreement with his role in this plan.

"Och," I said to them both as I sat back in my chair.

We all ate the bread, the first I have had in a while. I completely missed the creamy butter, but the plain loaf was more than welcome. Duncan poured my bottle into the quaich, and he and Will would just drink from the other bottles along with me.

"The trick is to just let it flow down yer throat," he said to us both. "It is just liquid, but if ye start or stop drinking, yer going to taste it and begin to gag. Let it go!"

"Ye are really making this verra easy, sir," I said sarcastically and with fear of what we were about to do.

"One last piece of bread, and let it settle," he said. We followed his instruction, and both nodded to him as he said loudly, "Drink! And dinnae stop!"

We all tipped our vessels and drank. I saw Will spit out his claret at some point, but I just let it flow slowly down my throat as I sat the empty quaich on the edge of the desk. Duncan sat his empty bottle next to it. Then Will finally finished his bottle.

"Well done! Well done! I swear by Christ, Alex, ye were *meant* to be the next chief of Clan MacLeod!" Duncan said, proudly staring into my bleary eyes with his hands across the desk.

"Well done, lass!" Will said in agreement. His inability to finish his bottle showing all over his face and his shirt.

I smiled at both men and then looked back at my uncle as I fell back into my chair and said, "I am going to be sick."

"No! Look at me, lass! Ye willna!" Duncan pointed his fingers to his eyes, and I was not. I wanted to, but I was not.

"I am *not!*" I said back to him as I sunk further in my chair.

"Now, lass," he said as the effects of a bottle of claret started to hit us both, "ye just have to do this once more. Will, I will declare it done and ye and I will have to escort her out of the room, y'ken."

Will said, "Aye, sir."

"But Alex, to fulfill the task means ye may *not* stop drinking at any point and ye may *not* be sick in front of the clan. Lad, even if ye have to carry her out of the room, the minute she is done, she has fulfilled the task. Ye can retch it all about me or Will, but only after ye are out of the room. But ye will have fulfilled the task! Ye need to spend every waking minute from here on out drinking water—not ale, wine, or whisky. It willna hit ye as hard."

I stood for a moment but felt uncertain of my feet and sat back down in the chair as my head was as liquid as my insides.

"Och how I *love* ye, Duncan," I said, flat drunk and reaching for his arm.

"And this would be the last thing, Will," he said, ignoring my drunken affection. "Yer gonnae have *this mess* on yer hands after the fact."

They both laughed at me in my ridiculous drunken state as the claret hit me hard and fast. "Ye will need to work with Missus Gerrard to ensure ye have all ye need in yer chamber for her to recover, not only for her, but fer ye. She will need to be seen at breakfast and across the grounds during the following day and it will be yer responsibility to make it so."

"Aye, sir," Will said to Duncan as he pointed to me now stumbling around the desk to my husband so I could fall into his arms. My husband carried me to my bed after being sick at least once on him on the way.

I said, barely able to keep my eyes open, "I am verra sorry, Will."

My beautiful and supportive husband just said, "I will do it all again tomorrow fer ye, Lady MacLeod."

+++

Great Hall of Castle Dunmara–19 May 1767

- **Ceremony:** *Confirmation of Alexandra Flora MacLeod as Lady MacLeod of MacLeod, the 25th Chief of Clan MacLeod by her uncle, Duncan Baird MacLeod.*

Duncan smiled at me and turned to the room as he said, "I stand before ye all as the last living brother of Laird Graham Malcom MacLeod, to perform the oath and transfer of power to his niece and declared heir, Alexandra Flora MacLeod. I hope ye all have yer own glasses filled to celebrate this moment with us." Parts of the crowd seemed to cheer in anticipation, and others scrambled to fill their glasses and ale pots.

Turning to me, Duncan continued by saying, "Lady Alexandra Flora MacLeod, do ye understand the importance of the role and responsibility yer about to take?"

"My uncle, it is a daunting task indeed to follow our beloved laird, but I am here to serve Clan MacLeod. I made my commitment many months ago when I was named as successor and heir. I stand here this night to help us navigate the future before us all, to carry the influence of our clan across Scotland and beyond our shores, and I will do this by putting the members of this clan at the heart of every decision I make."

He smiled at me and nodded for me to step forward. "Alexandra, ye will need to follow in the tradition of Clan MacLeod and drink this bottle of claret directly in one pass from the ancient silver quaich of the clan chiefs that preceded ye fer over five hundred years," he said holding it above his head so that the room could see it.

As he started to fill the quaich, he said to me and the room, "Lady MacLeod, ye cannae stop and start. Ye must take it all in one pass and ye cannae be sick in front of this room to be chief of this clan. Do ye understand this ask?"

"Aye, I do, sir," I said, swallowing my own nervousness lingering in my throat. I wish I had asked what would happen to our succession plan if I failed in this task, but now it was too late. Duncan finished filling the quaich with the bottle and I told myself all I had to do was what I did last night. I have done all that they have asked in preparation for this moment, and I looked to Duncan and then Will, hoping they agreed that one of them would carry me out of here the minute I finished.

"Hold Fast, Lady MacLeod," Duncan said as he handed me the vessel.

"Hold Fast!" said the entire room.

I did just as I had the other day. I let it all run down my throat and only really swallowed at the last. I sat the empty quaich before a smiling Duncan and a cheering hall. I looked at everyone before me with my own smile and nodded to the room with respect and appreciation. I gave a quick, wide-eyed look to Will and Duncan that this had better end quickly.

"May I present to ye on this the nineteenth day of May, Seventeen hundred and sixty-seven, the Lady MacLeod of MacLeod, Alexandra."

The room cheered, and I stepped back on my heels. Duncan fulfilled the last of his duty and said quickly as he saw my initial retreat, "Please enjoy the drink and fine food Missus Gerrard has provided us on this occasion in celebration of our new clan chief."

William placed his arm beneath mine and, unlike the night before, helped me get to our chamber, this time without incident.

+++

"This has to be the worst succession plan ever," I said, trying to catch my breath after heaving over a chamber pot for the second time.

"Ye could have been asked to raise a lifting stone *and* down a bottle of claret," Duncan said.

"How do ye feel, love?"

"Like I am drunk, but not bad. I thought if I could make myself sick, I would feel better and I do and yet, I dinnae."

Duncan said, handing me a slice of dry bread, "Here, eat more." I sat silently for a moment before he asked, "Can we get ye out there a bit more, lass?"

Will and I just looked at him like he was raving mad. And he had to be to ask such a thing of me sitting on the floor eating bread and drunk on claret. I could only thank God that I survived what was expected and was now comfortable and safe in my bedchamber.

"Breakfast will be fine," he said, "but what a feat for a woman to be seen at the end of the evening! Graham didna even do that!"

We all looked at each other now and I nodded that I think I could make it. Duncan clapped his hands and stood up before helping me off the floor.

"Aye! Will and I will stay close, but the minute ye feel sick, ye tell us, and we will take ye away. Being sick now doesna change anything from the ceremony, but we want to protect ye in front of members of the clan."

"Aye, sirs," I said, agreeing because as much as I would like to debate it, this could impress some people opposed to a woman as clan chief. The irony of such a feat is not lost on me.

"And remember ye have to be at the head table fer breakfast," he said.

"Ye mean dinnae drink anymore."

"Aye, people will want to give ye more in celebration, so toast with them. Sip, but dinnae drink."

"I *love ye so much* fer taking care of me," I said to them both, almost bleary-eyed.

"Och, Will," Duncan said, almost regretting his ask, "are ye ready fer this, lad?"

"Aye sir," he said as I believe they both laughed at me for a moment. I deserved it in my ridiculously drunken state.

"Here we go," Duncan said, ushering us out of our chamber back to the Great Hall.

+++

I made it through the evening and may have even won over some men in our clan with my endurance. I was clearly drunk, but not sick. I took Duncan's advice and only sipped or pretended to sip the drinks offered me. Nearly every person I talked to seemed to be in the same state I was in. I doubt they will remember much of me this evening. I knew I had to make it to breakfast and for the first time in a long while, looked forward to it.

I had an extensive conversation with Angus that I am convinced neither of us will ever remember. It may or may not have been about the technique of drinking a bottle of claret all at once and his admiration that I managed to do so.

I caught Will at some point and said with my arms around his neck, "If ye love me at all, ye will have already asked Missus Gerrard about fried ham and tatties."

He grabbed me by the waist and kissed me. Leaning into my ear, he said, *"Ye will have both delivered to our bedchamber before breakfast in the Great Hall."*

"Ye *do love* me," I said, drunk on claret and the night and kissing him all over his face.

"I love ye with all of my heart, Lady MacLeod," he said, laughing at my drunken spectacle.

"I believe I have hit my limit, sir. Please take me to bed."

"Ye will *never* have to ask me that more than once," he said as he smiled, lifted me up, and carried me to the back stairs to our bedchamber. Despite a room full of people, I kissed his neck and cheek all the way there.

+++

Duncan, Will, and I sat at the head table together, staring at the MacLeod kinsmen before us that could find their way to breakfast after a night of ceremony and celebration. Every one of them looked as pale and fragile as us. I kept telling myself that had I not secured my fried breakfast from Missus Gerrard, I would be under this table, though I could barely eat a thing on my plate at this point.

Duncan said, "One last item fer ye, my lady."

"Och Christ above! *What now?*" I asked, wondering what other feat I was going to have to perform to prove my worthiness.

"Calm yerself, lass! We have to move ye to the laird's, erm, I mean, to the new bedchambers and there are some question about the bed itself."

"Aye, I would verra much like my own bed placed in the chamber and our things delivered there as well."

I also could not think about sleeping in a bed or trying to make a family in a bed that both my aunt and uncle died in. I did not want to say those words aloud to Duncan, but believe he understood the thinking behind my response. Will smiled at me as we both knew the honest truth of it—*my bed was bigger.*

+++

TEN
In Due Time

Dunmara Castle
Isle of Skye, Scotland
May 1767

Robbie had Munro tacked for me and another horse for him and his mother to ride together. I nuzzled the face of my beloved horse while Robbie helped his mother mount theirs.

"Good morning, Auntie Sarah," I said as we were all settled in the courtyard.

"Aye Lady Alexandra, good morning to ye!"

We are destined for Dunmara Village this day to secure wee Robbie's spectacles from Doctor Norman, who visits Skye once a month from Glasgow. Auntie Sarah also wanted to buy some new linen to make her growing boy a new shirt. Our trip gives us a chance to spend even more time with each other. While part of our family, Sarah often keeps to herself, and sadly, we sometimes forget about her. Today, I am happy to spend some valuable time with both her and her son on my own.

+++

The doctor fitted Robbie with a small pair of wired spectacles, and he looked embarrassed to be wearing them at first. He kept moving them before his eyes.

"I ken that it will take some time to get used to having them before ye, but look at this paper. Can ye see the letters better, lad?"

"Aye, I can!" the lad exclaimed, taking the spectacles on and off while looking at the paper the doctor gave him.

"Ye will only need them for schoolwork, reading, and writing. I dinnae think ye need spectacles all day, and these are definitely not to be taken to the stables. Do ye understand, lad?"

Looking at Robbie now, I said, "It will be yer responsibility to care for yer new spectacles, do ye understand? Doctor Norman can tell ye best how to keep them clean and protected."

The doctor showed him how to clean them with a small linen cloth and gave him a leather case to keep them in when not wearing them. The boy no longer looked embarrassed with his spectacles. In fact, he looked quite proud of them. He would take them in and out of the small case and smile. Auntie Sarah and I only smiled at each other as we saw the confidence return to our sweet lad.

+++

After a small lunch together at the Old Stone on our way back through Dunmara Village, we finished our shopping in town just before returning to the castle. I waited for Sarah outside the shop, enjoying the pace of the village. It was a stark contrast to Edinburgh, but it was more crowded than the castle grounds. Watching the fishermen returning to the port was an event unto itself and made me happy.

"Here cousin," wee Robbie said, handing me a sealed parchment and breaking my trance with the harbor.

"What is this?" I asked as I broke the seal.

"I dinnae ken, another lad on the street asked me to bring it to ye," he said, looking around for the mysterious boy who was nowhere to be seen.

When I opened it, a gold chain fell out into my hand. A chain that could have been attached to a gold watch at some point. I could feel the panic and fear rise in my heart and my mind. The message was simple and ominous.

In due time

I looked around. Not for the lad who gave this message to Robbie, but the man who sent it—*Allan Calder*.

"Who gave ye this, Robbie?!" I asked him in a state of panic as I grabbed his shoulder.

"I told ye another lad. I dinnae see him now," he said, witnessing my panic and looking all around for the other mysterious boy.

This message and its contents were confirmation that Calder had my father's gold watch in his possession, and it was a warning to me. Calder was going to reveal himself again, *in due time*.

This was another threat, and it sent chills down my spine. I tried to collect myself in case the man was watching me from the shadows. I worried that he must have been watching me to know that I was in the village today. I did not want him to see me in a panic, though I clearly was. All I could do was rub the scars on my left wrist will my eyes looked at every person in the village in anticipation of the horrible and inevitable recognition of his face.

"Are ye alright, my lady? Ye have turned ghostly white and..." he said, touching my elbow, "yer scratching yerself."

In my panic, I was no longer rubbing the scars for strength and comfort. I was digging my nails into my flesh until the scars burned bright red.

"Robbie, I need ye to go inside and tell yer mother that it is time to go home." He just looked at me as I said loudly, *"Now, lad!"*

He was startled that I would speak to him this way, as I have never yelled at him in such a manner. But I am suddenly afraid that two women and a young boy are alone for the ride back to the castle. Before Edinburgh, it would not have been a concern. The village is close, and we know practically everyone on these lands, and they know me. The unknown is what has sent shivers down my spine.

Sarah came running down the steps of the shop with Robbie close behind. "Are ye alright, lass?"

"No Auntie, I am sorry to cut the day short, but we must return to the castle, and *now*."

"Did something happen?"

"I just need to talk with Duncan and Will right away on a clan matter," I said. Sarah and Robbie do not know what happened to me in

Edinburgh, and I am not going to explain it all here. I could feel the eyes of my tormentor on me, and while I could not see him, I would not give him the satisfaction of breaking down in the middle of the town square. I also needed us all to get to safe ground as fast as possible. Without my blade, we are vulnerable. I do not know if Sarah has one, but can only hope she does. Still, two women and a young lad would be easy targets on the road home.

We rode back to the castle together in relative silence. I handed Munro's reins to Robbie and said, "If Will is in the stables, send him to me straight away, lad."

With a swift tap on his neck, I left Munro for the first time without a single ounce of affection or gratitude. I felt horrible about it, but knew I would not be settled until I saw Will.

Robbie did not have to send in Will. I found the man looking for me in the Great Hall when I walked in. I grabbed him by the arm and said, "Come with me, *now!*"

He was clearly concerned by my frantic state as we climbed the steps to my chamber.

"What is this?" he asked.

He showed his concern even more so when we made it to the lady's chamber, and I slammed the door behind us before falling to my knees on the floor, gasping for air.

"Och, Christ above!" he yelled, trying to help me up as I trembled with fear and all that it took to return here without breaking down. "What has happened?"

I could not catch my breath enough to speak and finally had the strength to pull the ominous package out of my pocket to hand to him.

He looked over and asked quietly, "The gold watch?"

I nodded my head and finally said through my tears, "It is *Calder*! Will, what am I going to do? He is here! Calder is on Skye! I can *feel* it!"

"Hold on! Ye dinnae ken that," Will said softly and convincing neither of us with his calm and supportive assessment. "He could have sent this to be given to ye."

"He is *here*! I feel it and I have feared it for many months! What can *I* do?" What can *we* do?

"Ye are safe here in the castle. Ye are *safe here with me* now. But we need to talk to Duncan about our options to hunt the man on Skye. If he is here, he will be much easier to find than in the crowded city."

I nodded to him in agreement on this and welcomed the thought of resuming our hunt. Between Will, Angus, and Duncan, the man surely did not stand a chance. Part of me wondered why he would risk such a thing by coming here, but I feared him all the same.

"We will talk to Duncan after supper tonight. For now, I want ye to go to our bedchamber, wash yer face, and maybe rest for a bit. Will ye do that for me, my love?" I nodded to him as he continued, "Let me walk ye there. I promise it will be alright. *I promise!*"

I believed him because I am convinced, from this day he will probably never let me be alone again. But I am afraid of what was coming for us—what wickedness stands between me and my husband's promise.

+++

Will gave me a moment in our bedchamber. He went to find Duncan before supper and let him know what we would be asking of him. I locked the door to our room behind him. Even in the castle, I was consumed with fear without William with me. We got too comfortable in the MacLeod House on Canongate and now I could not become too comfortable at Castle Dunmara.

We ate our supper in silence. I scanned the room for any sight of the intruder. Much like when we returned to Skye, I felt he was bound to show himself and he has already proven that he can find his way in... undetected.

+++

"I dinnae question the ability of yer husband or the members of the clan to support ye here at Castle Dunmara. Look at me! Ye ken, that ye are safe here," Duncan said, holding my arm. I smiled weakly at him. I wanted to believe what he was saying to me, but I thought I was safe at MacLeod House as well.

In the brief time I was alone, my world crashed around me. Duncan knew the same and said, "But we all sadly ken too well what a few moments of weakness can mean. Ye took a risk going to the village with Sarah and Robbie alone, my lady."

I looked at him sharply, hurt by his words.

"I am not scolding ye and I wouldna have stopped ye. Not here! But knowing of this threat now, I need to ask Angus to protect ye when Will and I are not with ye. We are going to have to look at security once again."

I wanted to ask about getting my sgian-dubh back, but did not dare. I can see by the faces of Will and Duncan before me that Calder, possibly being on Skye, has unnerved us all. And I can see that they are afraid that

I may revisit feelings that made me harm myself. While I may feel like a prisoner in my own home, I almost welcome it... if it means I am safe. As much as I hate to admit it, they are right to keep me from my blade... for now.

+++

We settled into a regular rhythm of hand-offs between Angus, William, Duncan throughout the day. Mostly, Angus stood outside my chamber when I was not with my husband or meeting with Auld Knox and Duncan. What annoyed me on our journey to Edinburgh was now a welcome comfort each day.

"Good morning, Angus!" I said as Will and I walked to the lady's chamber. He just nodded his head to us and patted Will on the shoulder as we passed.

"Are ye joining me here this morning?" I asked Will as he assumed the security duty from Angus.

"Aye, if ye dinnae mind," he said. I could tell he had more to say to me and I waited. "Duncan and Angus are going to the village to look for Calder."

"They will kill him if they find him, Will." My words were as much a premonition as a fact. "I do not want them to be murderers on our lands. I will be forced as clan chief to deal with them, and not the vile Calder."

"No, dinnae fash! They ken to abide by yer orders. They will have him jailed even if he must be brought to the old dungeons here."

"Ye have discussed this, then?"

"Aye, I made it verra clear to them what ye said in Edinburgh applied here. And Duncan reminded us that ye are the law and justice on these

134

clan lands. If they find the man, he will be brought to the Great Hall for his crimes and punished accordingly."

I was annoyed at first that they were all planning this without me, but became relieved that they were honoring my wishes and my role as Lady MacLeod. I trusted them to look for Calder there, and I trusted them to look for him across Skye. I just do not know what any of us will do if we actually find the man.

ELEVEN

A Love Deserved

Dunmara Castle
Isle of Skye, Scotland
June 1767

Another summer is upon us, and the lads are already starting to arrive at Castle Dunmara. I have a meeting set with Master Knox and Master Harmon to prepare. We are all still learning our new roles and trying to work together without the benefit of the wise counsel of Laird Graham. I miss him every day. We have still not found the elusive specter of Allan Calder, but I know he just waiting and would find me... *in due time.*

"Sirs, I believe this summer will be much different from in year's past. Master Harmon, I am not sure if the laird mentioned to ye, but ye should expect to lose all of yer class this summer."

He looked confused and said, "No, Lady MacLeod. I did not know that. Why?"

"June and July bring upon important work for the clan on Skye. Ye have already seen some of this during lambing, where the children help their families during birthing season. Shearing is even bigger and young men will be tasked across the lands to support this effort."

"Second," I continued, "some of yer lasses are going to be sent to the treating of the wool, dying, waulking, and looming. And finally, we have a process that some lads and lasses are in training as apprentices in the kitchen, bakehouses, the forge, fishing, and the stables. These months are the most important to our clan lands in production and preparations that hold us for the year ahead. And they help our young men and women find a path for their future. Ye know that I believe academic education is essential, but education in *a life's work* is just as important. It is another key to survival on our clan lands."

He nodded to me on this in understanding as I continued, "We need to find ye an occupation, because ye will not have a class for the next few months, sir. I would always accept another pair of hands during this time, though I am also happy fer ye to return to yer home in England, if ye wish."

"I thank you, Lady MacLeod. I believe that I would like to return home to England." Master Knox and I looked at him as he continued, "My father died last month, and I should see about my mother. As their only child, my parents have been in receipt of some of my wages, but it would be a blessing to me to see how she is faring alone."

"Master Harmon, I had no idea," I said, walking around the desk to stand in front of him, my eyes showing genuine sympathy for his loss. "I am sorry to hear this news, sir!"

"Aye," Knox added, "I too am verra sorry for yer loss, sir."

Master Harmon just nodded to each of us with a weak smile.

"Ye should have let me ken. Perhaps we could have arranged fer ye to go home before now."

"No, Lady MacLeod, think nothing of it! It would have made no difference to the outcome. In some ways, I am glad to have missed the pain of watching him pass. However, this change for the summer will allow me to travel home and see to the care of my mother."

I could see that he was still in pain for the loss of his father and worried about his own mother's health and livelihood as a widow.

"Do what ye need for yer family, Master Harmon. My only ask is that ye please let us know if ye willna return to Dunmara as I will need to plan for a replacement. I dinnae want to lose any of the incredible progress ye have made here."

"Oh, no Lady MacLeod. I *will* return. I am happy here and believe in yer mission for education."

"Then ye will be most welcome back! Master Knox, we will record that classes will end on Friday and Master Harmon, ye are free to go any time after. Please go when it suits ye. We can confirm in the next Great Hall that classes will restart in the middle of August."

"That is the same start I had last year," Master Harmon said as he stood to leave.

"It will also give us a chance to determine who will be in yer new classes. So, if I may ask before ye leave, let us know how ye are evaluating yer students and whether ye can take on more. I will confirm, but believe we are just looking at two or three more new students—the youngest. I also want to ensure that I have yer home address so that I can send to ye any thoughts by letter in advance of the new school year."

I thought about how much progress we made together since my return to Skye, the awkwardness of us working together, and an unfortunate, and misguided kiss. Master Harmon has learned more about our home here on Skye and has become less of an English outsider. I know we both hated losing school for the summer, but I could not keep these children from learning in another way or from the needs of the clan.

Master Harmon shook Knox's hand and then nodded to me. "I will provide you with my evaluations before I leave, Lady MacLeod," he said as he walked out of the room.

I returned to my chair and said to the man sitting opposite me, "Master Knox, it is just us, sir!"

"Aye, my lady! It is just us."

+++

Master Knox and I stood together in the courtyard watching the activity of the lads arriving and the lasses being directed by Missus Gerrard. The activity is, at best, controlled chaos. I am confident in both of the Gerrards to lead the teams at the center of the summer operations.

At once, I spotted Grant and walked to him with a huge smile. This is the first time we have seen each other since I returned to Dunmara as a married woman, and he was a most welcome sight. I am not certain if he did not respond to my letter telling him that Will and I married, or if he did it not arrive to MacLeod House on Canongate before we left Edinburgh.

"My friend," I said, walking to him with my arms held wide.

He hugged me tight and said the same, "My friend."

"I have missed ye, sir."

"I am so verra happy fer ye, Alex! Erm, I mean Lady MacLeod." He held me tight in his arms for a moment and asked, "Where is Will? I want to tell him the same and shake his hand."

"I believe he is in the stables, and I ken he will want to see ye," I said, smiling at him and thinking of all the changes that have happened for us in the last year.

"Ye ken I had to go home to help settle things after my father died?"

"No! No one told me! I am so sorry, Grant!" I said, taking his hand. "I wondered where ye were. I worried that ye didna get the permanent position ye hoped fer."

"Aye, I got the permanent position in the forge and had to leave just two weeks later. It was difficult. The realization that I have no family anymore. But I am so grateful to be back at Dunmara."

"Och, Grant! We have much to talk about."

I thought about Will, Grant, and myself having no parents and feeling alone. I thought about Duncan feeling alone. I yelled to my auburn-headed cousin running through the courtyard inspecting horse after horse and said, "Robbie, go tell Will to join me at Cairn's Point!"

"Aye, my lady!"

"Let us go talk a bit, friend," I said to Grant, hoping that we could connect together a little more before Will arrived.

+++

"Yer happy for me, then?"

"Of course I am," he said as he hugged be tight with his left arm around me.

"Grant, I could have never abandoned my desire to be alone for anyone other than William MacCrimmon."

He looked at me in a way I did not expect but said, "I suppose not, my lady."

"Why do ye say that? And stop calling me, *lady*!"

"No reason at all, *Alex*," he said with a broad smile and a kiss on my cheek, "other than the man has been in love with ye most of yer life!"

"Stop it!"

"Aye, lass! He has told me for many years."

"And ye said nothing to me?!"

"I kent that ye didna want to marry, so why would I tell ye that someone loved ye? And why would I hand you another when I did love ye?"

"That isna fair! Ye have rejected me time and again because ye are not the *love I deserve,* but ye wanted to keep love from me?"

"Aye, I have been a horrible friend to ye," he said, laughing at me for a moment, "but it wasna about keeping love from ye. It was about making sure ye have the love *ye deserve.* Ye ken those have been my words from the verra start."

141

Those have been his words and his goal from the start, but I always saw it as a rejection of me and now my friend is telling me that he was looking for me to have what he could not provide.

"Aye," I said, in agreement, but still slightly confused.

"Then ye need to ken that I wanted the man to *prove* he was the love ye deserve—not just declare it to me—but to ye. When he showed his love defending yer honor with Wes, I kent he was deserving. But I also needed to see ye were willing to accept him, otherwise I feared I would scare ye off with the truth of his feelings."

"Will *is* the love I deserve. It has not always been easy for either of us. Ye ken my responsibilities are different here, and I am fiercely independent. We have had some struggles, but I ken that Will loves me as much as I love him."

Grant nodded to me but seemed to know I was holding back, and I was. He has no idea what happened in Edinburgh and what I have been through, but I could not say the words here—even though I wanted to tell my friend everything. This was not the moment to tell him the truth. I also do not want to relive the pain and fear of Calder. I just want to connect with my beloved friend.

"Are ye happy here?"

"Aye, much like Will, I have no family and nowhere else to go. I appreciate being given the opportunity to create my own future in the forge here at Dunmara."

"Och, Grant!" I leaned into him. I welcomed his words and his embrace.

"And I have found my own love." I pulled back and just looked at him, confused as he said, "Callum."

He could see that I could not place the name, and finally said, "Morrison, lass."

I know that my look back to him was shocked and when I could finally speak asked, "Morrison? The healer?"

"Aye, he is my love, and I am his."

"Then I am happy fer ye both, my friend," I said, hugging him, though I felt like my heart did not match my words. In fact, it was like Will confessed to me on the edge of our bed in Edinburgh—my heart was lifted and broken at the same time.

I have loved Grant MacAskill since I was six years old, before I even knew what romantic love was. To see us both matched with another deserving of our love should be a blessing, but his words still hurt me.

His words *did* hurt me.

+++

"Och, Grant!" Will yelled over the cliff as he joined us. They shook hands and Grant congratulated Will on our marriage. Grant made a joke to him about knowing it was destined. I smiled, knowing that my friends had their own secrets, and that Grant was just another that could see what I could not.

Seemingly done with the heartfelt connections, Grant asked, "Should we assume our positions back on the stone wall and watch the events in the courtyard?"

We all agreed and walked down to the stone wall together. Much like the year before where we sat together talking of Gillies MacBane and the incoming lads, we observed the new lot returning for the summer. I sat

143

between the only two men I have ever loved in my life and smiled to myself that we were all friends—*forever* friends.

+++

My husband, however, was not as content as I was with our reunion, and the ugly head of male jealousy roused in him once again when we arrived at our bedchamber before supper. His face and his angry silence told me everything he was thinking. We have had this conversation before. I knew exactly what was coming my way and braced myself for it.

"*Will!* Please stop this. Grant has no interest in me beyond being my friend."

"Ye are so blind, lass," Will said dismissively.

"Insult me as ye wish, but Grant is not interested in the company of a woman—*any* woman."

He looked at me for a moment and I stared into his eyes, willing him to understand until he did.

"He is a Sodomite, then?" Will asked, almost uncertain of his own words.

I knew the term, but it was not one that I would use on my own and just nodded. He seemed shocked about both the thought of Grant in the company of another man and maybe the fact that I knew the truth of it.

"Did ye ken, Alex?"

"Aye, I have kent fer a few years."

My husband said nothing to me. I confessed everything to him as I held him tight in my arms.

"Will, I loved Grant as a young lass and I couldna understand why he didna love me back the way I thought he should." I looked up at him as a flash of recognition of his own similar feelings crossed his face. "Aye! Ye ken how *that* feels!"

"Aye, I do," he said softly and nodded his head in understanding and remembrance of loving me when I did not feel the same toward him. I did not say a word to him about it, but I learned with Will what it felt like to hurt another, not loving them the way—or when—they wanted. It told me everything Grant felt for years, and it broke my heart.

"We have known each other since I was just six years old. It is not even about romantic love. We bonded as friends first, with his kindness to help me when I fell in the courtyard and then over the loss of our mothers. That fact will *never* change. Grant is the first friend I ever had in my life!"

He held me tight as I continued, "We had an awkward moment a few years ago."

I worried about what Will would think, but was happy that I could continue to show him my heart and tell him the truth of it all. "I tried to kiss him after one of his incredible stories up at Cairn's Point and he refused me. It was difficult to accept the open rejection from my dearest friend. *He broke my heart.*"

"All this time, ye never told me."

"It never came up. I mean, other than when I told ye that I had heartbreaks that made me feel like that I didna deserve love."

"Grant?"

"Aye, Grant."

He nodded in understanding and let me continue, "As embarrassing as that moment was fer me, I believe it was one of the reasons I decided that I would *never* marry. He hurt me so that I told myself that I never wanted to feel that way again. So, I decided at that verra moment that it was easier to reject something outright than to let someone that close again and break my heart into a million pieces. As time passed, it became easier and easier to say that I didna want the one thing I felt I was deprived of. It hurt less that way. I gained some sort of false confidence in my own independence by such a declaration, but it was nothing. It was a weak declaration made out of *pain and fear*."

"And when I saw ye both at Cairn's Point that night after the Great Hall?"

"Och, that was the second time he broke my heart," I confessed. Will looked confused as I tried to explain. "Grant tried to comfort me that night after the Great Hall with ye and Wesley. He said the same truth ye did, and I admired ye both fer protecting my honor and my virtue. *I did, my love!*"

Looking away from him, I confessed, "Then, I told him I wished he would just marry me and take me away from the rumors and speculation that would surely follow me the rest of my days as an unmarried woman in a leadership position in the clan. I kent Wesley would not be the last man to try to dishonor me and tarnish my name or reputation for his own gain, and it made me afraid."

Will stepped back, and I walked to him, placing my hand on his chest. "When ye met me on my return to the castle, Grant had just told me that *couldna* happen. He remained true to the fact that he was not the love I *deserved*."

He took my hand and bent it to kiss my wrist and then me.

"*Will*," I said quietly. "I will tell ye what I told Grant that night. I said to him what did out of embarrassment and frustration at the situation with Wesley in front of the Great Hall. As much as I was hurt by what happened, I already knew his response, but I still said the words. I learned as I got older that it wasna me that he was rejecting and what I said was foolishness. Ye came upon us after Grant told me that he loved me, but could never love me the *way I deserved*. So ye need to ken that he is a friend, one that I love with all of my heart, but Grant is no challenge to ye. Yer the man that loves me the way I deserve. Grant just kent it before I did." I kissed him on the cheek and as I pulled back to look him in the eyes, they seemed suddenly softer and bluer.

Will hugged me and said into my ear, *"I am sorry I challenged yer friend."*

"Our friend!"

"Aye, *our friend.* Ye ken I went to Grant about what Wes was saying, because I respected and trusted him as a friend."

"I ken that. I do, Will. Please dinnae say anything to anyone else."

"I will not, but some lads on the clan lands already ken the truth. That is all I will say."

"Ye mean there have already been rumors?"

"Aye, there have been rumors about a few lads over the years, but it never changed my opinion. I havena seen anything from him other than friendship, so took the rumors fer nothing more than that—*rumors*. Being here permanently at Dunmara could expose him more. Does he ken that?"

"I hope he does, but I have not talked to him about it. We only talk about his life in halting words. But he confessed to me tonight that he and Master Morrison are together."

"Morrison? *The healer?*"

"Aye. *Please Will*, I need yer help! He is my oldest and dearest friend. We must protect him. We must protect *them both*."

"Aye, love," Will said in a voice that did not sound completely convinced but followed my lead as his wife and as Lady MacLeod.

TWELVE
The Other Woman

The Great Hall was louder than usual with the arrival of the lads of summer. It made the room and atmosphere feel exciting and festive. Many remained after supper, catching up with each other and enjoying the plentiful food and drink Missus Gerrard had on offer. I surveyed the room from the corner and thought about how much I always loved this time of year.

Duncan walked forward with his new love. Will and I stood before them, interested to know more about the woman who had kept my uncle from us for so long. I tried to keep a smile on my face, though I was not particularly impressed from the start.

"Lady MacLeod and Master MacCrimmon," Duncan said quite formally, "may I introduce ye to Missus Charlotte Harold?"

Before we could say anything, the woman said with her words dripping with sticky honey sweetness, "Aye, it is my pleasure to meet ye Alexandra and Master MacCrimmon... *finally*! I told my dearest Duncan that he couldna hide me away from ye *forever!*"

She knew that she should have recognized me as Lady MacLeod and she did not, but I let it go for a moment. I knew that Missus Harold was a widow on our lands, but nothing else. I did not recognize her and did not know if she had any children from her previous marriage. She was not at all what I expected from Duncan. This is the same man that told me once that he was one who could not settle with one woman. It was a mark of change for him to settle down and introduce me to another woman. It was an unexpected change for us, and I am not sure I like it.

Missus Harold was tall like us, but much heavier, but it was her demeanor that stood out. Her false sweetness was laced with an air of entitlement. Perhaps she felt like her relationship with Duncan elevated her status in the Great Hall. Her dress was made of all sorts of blues and greens, not to mention an unnecessary amount of lace and ribbons. She had a rose in her hair that made me think of my mother, and I resented her instantly for it. I could tell that Charlotte Harold was not what she appears to be.

Will shook Duncan's hand and nodded his head to the woman, saying, "It is a pleasure, Missus Harold."

I looked at Duncan and wondered what '*hide her forever*' meant, but I had no thoughts other than what I felt in the moment. I dislike this woman. I know it was not fair to judge in such a short amount of time, but that was truly my first thought.

I dislike this woman!

"Missus Harold, it is a pleasure to meet ye," I said as cordially as I could. I smiled at Duncan, and he smiled back but the exchange was awkward and uncomfortable. I am sure my true thoughts showed on my face... as they always do. I took Will's hand and walked him to the other side of the room, away from them both after our introductions. I was in no mood to try to have a conversation with Duncan or Missus Harold this night. I just wanted to get as far away from them as I could.

"Are ye alright?" Will asked me in a whisper.

"No! I am not!"

"Love," he started to say before I interrupted him.

"It is fine. I just needed a moment. Thank ye for walking here with me."

Will said nothing, but kissed me quickly on my cheek. He knows what I am feeling without the words, and he was more than happy to help me escape an uncomfortable moment.

I finally left Will's side to refill my glass and when I turned around to survey the room, Missus Harold came to stand next to me and said, "May I have a word?"

"Of course, Missus Harold."

She turned from standing next to me at the table to standing before me. After taking a sip of her own glass, she said, "I would verra much like to get along with ye, lass. It is important to me and *my beloved Duncan.*"

Her face was stern, and yet her voice was sickly sweet. The two did not match each other. And much like my last interaction with the haunting shadow, Allan Calder, I forgave the one transgression by using *lass as a sneering insult.* I would not be as forgiving on a second.

I said dismissively over my glass, already annoyed, "I just met ye, Missus Harold. I am not certain there can be any indication of *getting along or not*."

"As a woman I can tell ye dinna want to get along, lass."

"Ye ken nothing about me or what I want, madam," I said as a matter of fact.

"Well then, let me say that fer us to get along, ye should not be so dependent on yer uncle, lass," she said. Surely, she knows who she was talking to. And this is her third *lass*. "While I am at it, I also dinnae care fer the way ye speak to him. It isna respectful or becoming fer a young woman to speak to a man so."

Again, I am the Lady MacLeod and just met the woman minutes ago. I have absolutely no idea how she knows how I speak to Duncan, so I tried to ignore her admonishment and correction.

"No, missus. It has nothing to do with *dependence*. The man is my uncle *and* my friend," I said as she scoffed, which only enraged me more. "And ye should ken by now that *my uncle* is the guardian of my trust until I turn twenty-one. It is his *responsibility*."

She stepped closer to me and said, "With me, Duncan will only have *one responsibility*, lass."

That is her fourth—and final—*lass*.

"Lady MacLeod."

She looked startled that I was so abrupt with her, but she has crossed a line. Not since Mean Old Mary MacAskill have I ever dealt with such a bitter and disrespectful woman.

"What?"

"Like it or not, I am yer *lady*, not yer *lass*. Ye will address me properly, Missus Harold."

I left her standing there, mouth open and fuming that I would speak to her so. She had no words but was clearly unhappy with my point of correction or even the way I said her name. Though I admit that I was more than satisfied with her response. I just smiled to myself as I walked back to find Will. I passed Angus and Duncan and refused to look at or speak to either of them. They could tell by my face and the fuming woman that walked slowly behind me that our conversation had not gone well.

"*Christ above!*" Duncan said under his breath as I passed him, took my husband's hand, and led him to our bedchamber to end our night.

+++

We started to undress in silence. I could not even look at him. I was so consumed with my own anger. He could feel the icy chill in my hands and my demeanor when I escorted him from the Great Hall and he remained silent, waiting for me to speak when I was ready.

"What do we think of Missus Harold?" I finally asked.

Will smiled at me and knew the game we were about to play, and he knew precisely what I thought of the woman. "I dinnae ken! What *do we think* of Missus Harold, love?"

"She is the foulest woman I have ever met! That is what I think!"

"Could it be that ye are jealous of her?"

"*Jealous!*? How could ye say such an outrageous thing to me?"

"Not of the woman *that way*," he said, coming to help me with my laces. "He is yer uncle, but he is also yer friend, and he has directed his

153

attention suddenly to someone else... another woman... and I think ye miss him."

"I get yer meaning."

I sat on the edge of the bed dressed in my shift and thought about his words. Perhaps I am jealous that this woman has taken my most trusted friend and uncle from me, and I ken that the tension I have felt with Duncan of late is because we have been apart more than ever before.

I do miss him.

I walked to Will and put my arms around him. "I think yer right."

He leaned back as if this were a momentous confession. And maybe it was. He said with a smile, "I would verra much like ye to say *that* again. I only regret no one else is in the room to hear it!"

He made me laugh as I said again loudly, *"Och, my love! I think yer right!"*

"That is more like it," he said with a quick kiss on my cheek.

"Glenammon had already taken him from us, but aye, I *am* jealous of the time he is spending with her. There is more, Will. I dinna like Missus Harold in *any way!*"

"Come now," Will said. He has always been so good at trying to calm me and settle my emotions. It is another reason he is such an incredible partner to me.

"No, sir! I dinna like *anything* about her as a woman and fer Duncan to be so in love with someone I find so *dreadful,* makes me want to retch!"

Will gave me a look, and I immediately tried to correct myself. "I mean, it makes me sad. Sad that someone like that would come between us."

With him still staring at me, I tried once again to correct myself, "Aye! I am jealous, but I am mostly lamenting this complete waste of our time and emotion for a woman that does not deserve him."

"Come now, *my love*."

"I dinnae want to hurt him, but this has been a difficult change for us."

"*I ken,*" Will said softly in my ear as he rocked me a bit in his embrace.

"I have to support him as he supported ye. Ye ken he supported ye, Will. In fact, Duncan loved and supported ye as a match before I did. He could see what I could not—or what I *would* not."

"Och, my love," he said, kissing my forehead.

"I cannae say the same for Missus Harold. I dinnae trust her and I believe she is after his money from Glenammon, *and* she was disrespectful to me. Not just my position as Lady MacLeod, but as his niece. She was clear in her choice of words, telling me that I was too dependent on the man, and that she did not appreciate the way Duncan and I speak to each other."

"She did? That seems bold, considering she just met ye."

"Aye, exactly! She did! I have no idea how she formed such an opinion of me unless he said something to her. We are not formal with each other, that is true. And when either of us have been truly disrespectful, we always tried to correct ourselves and apologize."

"Aye, ye have."

"Then she let me ken that without question, he has only *one responsibility*, and that is to *her*. Will, the woman, has a completely different demeanor away from Duncan, which is a sign to me that she is not honest or truthful. She is all sweetness and light in front of him, but she was cold as ice and disrespectful to me when we were alone. I swear to Christ! If she called me *lass* one more time!"

"I ken how ye feel about that!" Will shook his head in disbelief that Missus Harold would say such a thing and his own understanding that the dismissive use of the term *lass* makes me irate.

"So, finally, I told her that I was her lady, not her lass, and her face turned purple! I bet she has never had anyone talk to her that way, but like it or not, she will address me appropriately. *She is not my family!*"

"Not yet anyway!"

I turned to him sharply, and he just tilted his head to me. He was correct that it could be a possibility if Duncan marries this horrible woman. She is most likely leading him in that direction by the looks of it. The mere thought of such a thing would be tragic for our family and potentially destroy my relationship with my uncle.

"Dinna say that, Will," I said, hoping that this woman will never be part of our family. I walked away from him and sat before the fire.

Will joined me and wrapped his arms and legs around me like we used to at Glenammon House. He kissed the back of my head and said, "She may be after his money, but what can ye do about it?"

"I dinnae ken"

"Ye ken he is his own man and is as stubborn as ye are when challenged. He will not take yer resistance to his new love well. Ye heard him curse under his breath when ye left the room. *And* ye can expect he is getting a mighty earful from the woman at this verra moment."

I just nodded. Will was right again. There would be no way to confront Duncan on this topic without putting him square in the middle of the two women he loves.

I sat in silence for a moment and then turned my head back to look at Will. "I can help him see what I do. He helped me see what I could not with ye. Perhaps as a woman I can see things he cannae in this case."

We sat silently for a moment, and I continued my thought, "I want Duncan to find love like I have, but I dinnae want him to love someone that openly and willingly drives a wedge between the two of us. That is what this woman is trying to do. She made her intentions verra clear to me in our conversation. My uncle would be appalled if he heard her speak to me the way she did this night."

Will remained quiet on my words, but held me tighter. As I thought more about it, I said, "I have to believe that at some point, Duncan will resist a woman that makes me her enemy."

"Aye, my love! I cannae see that ending well for anyone if that is her intention."

+++

Duncan stopped eating with us at the head table so that he could sit with Missus Harold for meals instead. Each day that passed, I became more and more angry. I took his decision, likely rooted in nothing but love and romance, to be offensive because of the woman involved. She did nothing to correct her behavior after the night we met, and he was blatantly choosing her over his family and his responsibility to this clan.

From what I can see, Charlotte Harold also relishes flaunting his decision before me as she noisily holds court at her own version of the *head table* on the opposite side of the Great Hall.

He has also talked to me less because he knew when Will and I walked out of the hall without a word to him and the look on my face, what I thought of his new love. He does not need to me to confirm it for him. He knows better than to bring it up to me, so he avoided me as much as I avoided him.

Duncan knows that out of courtesy for my position as clan chief and head of our family, he will have to ask my permission to marry the woman. Thankfully, he has not come to me for that. I do not know what I would do if he did. One thing for certain is that I missed the man terribly. My uncle was as much my friend as my family, and not speaking to him was a torment for me. He was already absent because of the brewery and distillery, but now we could not even have supper together because of this horrible woman.

"Yer anger is showing, love," Will whispered to me at the head table as I stared at Duncan and Missus Harold on the other side of the room, unable to eat what was on my plate.

"Thank ye. There is indeed an icy chill in the air this night."

I tried to relax my face, look anywhere but in the direction of their table, and eat my supper. Instead, I retreated to my old habits of seeking to control what I could, and I just moved food from one side of my plate to the other as I stared at their table. I sat my cutlery to the side of my plate and said softly and honestly to Will, *"I miss him."*

"I ken ye do, and I believe the man misses ye just as much. When yer ready, ye should talk. I understand that yer avoiding conflict fer now, which is fine, but nothing will ever be resolved without talking."

I kept staring forward, though the tears were clearly forming in my eyes. "I hoped it would all just end and we could avoid all of this. I fear he willna listen to me."

"He *loves* ye, that I ken well enough," Will said, grabbing my hand in his, immediately forcing the tears in my eyes to fall one by one onto my cheeks. "He may not agree with ye in the end, but he will listen to ye."

"Aye, my love," I said softly.

Will was right again. I would have to find the right time and the right words for that conversation to happen. I would also have to find the right attitude and I am not ready...not yet.

THIRTEEN
Knights Of The Realm

Dunmara Castle
Isle of Skye, Scotland
June 1767

Duncan sat across from me in my chamber but said nothing. He clearly did not like my decision to pull all the new lads to finish the shearing and to remove the few I had originally allocated to Glenammon. He is not alone in his losses, as I had to pull the lads that were allocated to the stables and forge as well. His face told me that he not only disagreed, but was angered by my decision.

"Ye are not looking at this the right way, Alex!" he said, challenging me fully.

"Why do you get a voice here in my decision with Master Knox on how we allocate the summer lads?" I yelled louder than I should have.

"Why is your first response always in the form of a question?"

The general dismissiveness in his words, within a game he knows frustrates me, set my blood boiling! I could feel it, and this was not going to be good for either of us. My frustration with him clearly showing, Auld Knox knew enough to walk away from my chamber. Duncan and I were left alone in our silence.

"I am sorry to say this to ye, my lady, but yer not looking at the long-term implications of such a decision."

"No sir because I am looking at the short-term implications here. I am already at a deficit on the lads on our lands, so much so that I am forced to train lasses to shear sheep, not just treat the wool. Yer brewery, while a focus, is a secondary one, fer now. Ye will have to lead on the clan lands in many ways in yer role. In fact, I could use ye here and not Glenammon, but I willna ask ye to choose."

"This is not a good decision!"

"Ye forget yerself! I dinnae *need* yer advice on these topics I have already cleared with my estate factor," I said with the false confidence of a young woman filled with frustration at being challenged and directing it to the one person that did not deserve it—at least not fully. Since meeting his new love, our relationship has been strained. We are not happy with each other, yet kept pushing the limits of our own patience while refusing to have the one conversation we actually should.

"Laird Graham taught me well. I am the chief of Clan MacLeod. It is my responsibility to protect our people and our lands. So I must be honest, I dinnae see what value yer current counsel provides for me on this topic. It appears all ye have to offer me is correction in service to yer own personal interests and I find that... *distasteful*."

I stood up from my chair and met his eyes as we were nearly the same height. I could tell he was disappointed in me for being so disrespectful, but in typical fashion... I did not stop talking.

"I think ye should tend to yer business and let me tend to mine. I dinnae have the time or the inclination to fight ye, sir! *It is exhausting!*"

I immediately closed my eyes in regret for the words I said aloud. In a moment of being challenged, I fought back cruelly and sought to hand off my anger and pain at someone who loves me, and I him. This is not how we should be with each other. Turning to him in immediate remorse for my words, I said softly, "*Uncle...*"

"No, lass! Erm, my lady, I agree with ye. I cannae imagine my counsel is any help to ye now that ye have taken such *responsibilities*," he said stoically and yet with some derision. Some well-deserved derision. "But family is family. Like it or not, I will always be here for ye if ye need me, and I will always tell ye the truth. I made a vow to yer mother. I made a vow to yer father. I made a vow to Laird Graham. Solemn vows that only death will break. I respect yer ask of me to step aside, but ye can never make me break my vows!"

Seeing the tears starting to form in my eyes, Duncan took my hand in his and said with a sly smile and a wink, "*Like it or not*, ye are stuck with me, lass... *and I am stuck with ye!*"

His frustration and his own pain were apparent in his last words. He let go of my hand, kissed me on the forehead, and walked out of the room. I could barely hide my smile through my tears. Despite my feeble attempt, Duncan would not let me be an insolent child, no matter how hard I tried.

This poor man was stuck with me, indeed!

+++

It was late, and I needed to go to bed, but I missed supper while spending time checking everything on the map and hoping that we were set for the reallocation of the summer lads in the middle of the season. I also wanted to see again if there was anything I could spare for Glenammon. Despite arguing with Duncan, I still wanted to see if I could help him.

Then it came to me! I could see if some of the older lads looking for permanent placement might be willing to work at Glenammon in the evenings. It is something I had not considered before, or I would have offered it to Duncan as a compromise when we met earlier.

I knew Missus Gerrard would have bread and butter in the kitchen for me to take to my chamber. I relieved Angus from his security watch earlier, thinking I would go to my bedchamber earlier than I did. I had not seen Will since the morning and, based on the current state of security, he would soon be looking for me. He would be disappointed that I was alone in my chamber for so long.

I walked out of my chamber mindlessly, exhausted from the day. I walked downstairs through the Great Hall when I saw Angus out of the corner of my eye. He was chatting with a small group of men in the back of the room. It was unusual to see him without Duncan. His eyes caught mine and narrowed for a moment. Perhaps it crossed his mind that I was walking through the castle alone, but he quickly turned back to his audience. They were having a grand time laughing and drinking.

I went straight to the kitchen to see what Missus Gerrard had left from supper. When I turned around with buttered bread in my mouth, Angus was standing right before me. I jumped back quickly, as he was just a tad too close. I am not certain how I did not smell him first, as he absolutely reeked of sweat, whisky, and his horse all the time. But there the man was!

"Och, Christ above!" I said as I stepped back slightly and put my hand over my chest, nearly choking on the bread in my mouth.

"Haud yer wheesht!" he said with his finger in my face. Angus seemed angry, as his eyes were blazing. I turned my head to look at him sideways in anticipation of his words. If I could understand them, that is.

He remained quiet for too long, so I asked, "Something on yer mind, man?"

"Aye, 'tis something on mi' mind t'be sure," he paused to check his words, but he was clearly angry with me. "I dinnae think I would ever say th' words to ye," he said with sober conviction. In fact, I have barely understood a single word Angus has said since I have known him. "But I am sorrowful disappointed in ye, my lady."

The only topics that will get you this direct of a stare, serious tone, and to be honest, understandable words from Angus MacLeod are his recollection of the Battle of Culloden, the finer points of whisky, and that he believes he has the best horse on the Isle of Skye. Shadow is indeed a fine horse, but I dare not tell him the lad cannot compete with my Munro in any way!

My immediate reaction was belligerent and sarcastic as I looked above and said, "I ask God Himself, every night in my prayers... *how many fathers does one woman need in her life?*"

"Dismiss me as ye wish, *Lady MacLeod*. Or perhaps I sh' channel yer *fathers* and ask ye, *why is yer first response always a question?*"

He knew this would make me angry. Before I could argue with him, he continued, "But yer uncle—a fine and 'onest man sits drownin' 'imself in whisky an' sorrow at the Old Stone."

Despite my initial annoyance at being scolded in the kitchen by the man, I admired that our cousin was standing here before me, loyally defending the best friend he has in this life. I admired him for telling me the truth, and despite the scolding, I knew only one thing. I deserved every word.

"I hurt him today and I immediately regretted it, Angus. He tried to tell me something I didna want to hear. While I disagree with his position, I said horrible things to him out of frustration. I promise ye I didna mean the words I said or how I said them."

"Aye, he didna deserve it."

"He didna," I said softly, under my breath as I hung my head. Standing quietly for a moment, I thought about a solution and looked up and asked, "Angus, will ye escort me to the tavern?"

"Och, my lady. I am no' sure what state we will find 'im in. It is late, and I left 'im there over an 'our ago."

"I understand. We can decide when we get there if Duncan and I can speak but, I cannae go to bed tonight knowing that we parted the way we did. I recently learned that painful lesson with my own husband. Will ye help me, sir? Will ye escort me to the tavern?"

Almost in resignation, but also relishing his role as peacemaker and security watch, Angus said, "Ye get yer cloak, and I will get Shadow. I will meet ye in the courtyard."

I took my bread upstairs and placed it on my side table for later. I grabbed my cloak from the hook and told Will what had happened with Duncan and what Angus had said to me in the kitchen.

"I must right this wrong," I said as I kissed my beloved. "Like I promised ye, I cannae leave angry words between us or I will regret it forever."

"I should go with ye! It is late," he said as he started to get up from bed.

"No, stay here, my love," I said, brushing his dark curls away from his forehead before kissing him. "I will be with Angus. I will be safe."

He kissed me once more as he said, "I love ye."

"I ken ye do, and I love ye more!"

+++

We rode in relative silence to Dunmara village and the Old Stone Tavern. Despite his lack of hygiene... and decorum... and let's face it, general sobriety, Angus is a good man. He has proven more than once that he was not only a true and loyal friend to Duncan, but he was our family. And I trust him to keep me safe on our journey.

Once we arrived outside the tavern, he helped me dismount Shadow and I asked, "Angus, do ye want to have a look inside to see if Duncan is in a state to speak with me?"

"Och m'lady, I find in these situations, a surprise can sober ye up in a flash," he said, laughing as a man clearly speaking from experience. "But, aye, I will look fer ye."

I nodded as he peeked inside the door and, within a moment, came right back to me. The irony of Angus checking on the coherence of anyone else in a tavern was not lost on me. I just smiled at him when he returned at that very moment.

"The man is alone. He looks drunk but is awake and sittin' upright. Back table on th' right. Go to 'im and if ye cannae 'ave the conversation ye need, just bring 'im out and we will take 'im 'ome. Ye can right this wrong another time."

"Thank ye, Angus," I said as I touched him on the shoulder and smiled.

He seemed shocked for a moment at this kindness, and retreated back for a moment, but smiled back at me and said, "Ye two are the most stubborn members of our family, but I love ye both wi' all of my 'eart."

"Look at ye being sentimental! Pray fer me, sir!"

"Aye! Ye both need many prayers, lass! Erm, my lady," he said as he turned back to tend to Shadow. I watched him walk away, knowing he was right. We both needed prayers. I walked through the door and due to the hour, only the barkeep, Auld Jonah, noticed me. In fact, he seemed startled by my late arrival at the tavern, but glanced over at Duncan and realized immediately why I was here.

"Can I get a whisky, Jonah? Actually, make it two."

"Of course, Lady MacLeod. I will bring 'em over to ye."

I stopped in front of Duncan's table and said, "May I sit with ye, sir?"

It took a minute for my words to register. Angus was right. The art of surprise on increasing sobriety in an instant is worth more study. Duncan stood up immediately and put his arm around me to protect me. "What are ye doing here, lass? Ye should not be here alone this late in the evening!"

I smiled, knowing that his genuine concern went first to my personal safety. It was one of the things I loved most about him. I put my hand on top of his. "All is well. Angus escorted me here safely and is waiting for us both outside."

This was enough reassurance for him to slowly return to his seat. Before I could speak again, Auld Jonah brought our glasses of whisky to the table. Duncan and I were looking at each other silently for a bit. We both had much to say, but who would go first?

I raised my glass, and he eventually took the cue to meet his to mine.

"*Sláinte*," we said in unison, bringing this unofficial family meeting to order.

I leaned in, trying to meet his eyes. I extended my hand to his across the table as I said, "I owe ye an apology, Duncan. What I said today was unfair and how I said it was... *disrespectful*. I could not go to my bedchamber this night knowing that I talked to ye so. Can ye forgive me?"

"Och, lass," he just put his head down to his chest as his hand took mine in recognition of my apology and our bond as family.

He just kept his head low but could not find his own words. Finally he said, "I ken ye are not happy about Charlotte."

"That is not completely fair. Not untrue. But she is not why we quarreled or why I am here tonight. We can discuss Missus Harold another time."

He kept his head low. We could discuss Missus Harold another time when he has not had a night of whisky and I could find the words I need.

"I told Angus that I couldna bear to have our last words be what they were. Ye ken I learned that painful lesson with Will. I kent better and want to do better."

"Aye, lass."

"I have told myself that I could do this work for the clan on my own and I know that I cannae. My mother is gone. My father is gone. Laird Graham and Lady Margaret are gone. I *need* ye, Duncan. I *need* yer advice and counsel. I *need* yer love and support. And aye, sir! I even *need* yer correction when I am out of line. I return your words back to ye—*ye are stuck with me.*"

"Aye, and yer *stuck with me.*"

We finished our drinks, and as he placed his empty glass on the table, he said, "I have but one more thing to say." I just looked at him as we sat silently for a moment in anticipation of his words.

Finally, he spoke.

"I take my role as the last living member of the council of brothers seriously... maybe too seriously. Yer grown, lass and yer a natural leader. Ye also have a loving and capable husband to support ye. Ye are the Lady MacLeod and ye dinnae need my opinion or correction. I wasna being respectful of yer role and I was treating ye like a child."

"Duncan..." I started to say, but he did not let me finish.

"I will try to wait for ye to ask before I share my opinion. Ye have my commitment. I dinnae always ken what other things ye are balancing with the clan lands, and I was only looking to where I needed help, not at what ye were managing with Auld Knox fer the shearing. I apologize to ye."

"I thank ye, sir, but I dinnae think that is enough for me."

He seemed startled by my response, having just given in on restricting his advice and offering his own apology. He leaned back in his chair, waiting for my explanation.

"I think ye have a most important role, as my uncle, and as ye said, my *last* father. I never want ye to hold back yer opinion. That means I dinnae want ye to wait for me to ask for it!"

"Alexandra..." he started to say.

I interrupted his response and said after I collected myself, "I will tell ye that I rely on ye more than ye ken." I could feel the emotion rising in my throat, along with the tears in my eyes. "Duncan, ye can say things to me that no one else in this world can, and I am the same with ye. We are honest with each other in a way that is... *special* to me. It is important to me."

He put his chin to his chest and nodded at my words.

"Please tell me the truth, even if it is truth I dinnae want to hear, and I will do the same. That means that we will have many more disagreements in our lifetime. I only ask that we make a point to resolve our differences and that we speak the truth to each other with love and respect. Today, I did not offer ye that, but I will be better, sir."

"Ye have my commitment, lass."

"I have one more ask. I want ye to serve by my side, going forward in the Great Hall from this moment forward as the last of my fathers." He looked at me with surprise as I continued, "Sir, that means with all that ye have at Glenammon, I am asking ye to sit with me and Auld Knox to prepare for the Great Hall each month and stand next to me on the night. Ye didna ken what we were balancing across the clan lands, and I assumed ye did."

He smiled knowing I was asking him to be more than just the uncle, that I wanted him to be part of my decision-making and I reached across the table to take his hand again as I said, "I love ye, Duncan."

"I love ye, lass. More than ye ken."

"Also, I have been thinking about Glenammon. We could ask some of the older lads looking for permanent positions at Dunmara if they want to take on extra work in the evenings for ye. Ye may not have many volunteers, but there are some hardworking lads out there that will take the opportunity for additional pay and perhaps a future role after the shearing."

"That is a good idea, my lady! I can agree to that!" Duncan said, relieved at the compromise versus having no help at all.

"We have more to discuss to be truly honest with each other. But fer now, I think we should go home," I said as I stood up and put my hand out to lift him from his seat. Duncan knew immediately that neither of us was in a state to discuss Missus Harrold this night. We will just take one topic at a time. He stood and hugged me tight before helping me with my cloak.

Auld Jonah came around to our table to clear the glasses as I said, "Thank ye and please place this on my account, sir. Angus will come by tomorrow to settle it fer me. Fer now, we bid ye a good night!"

"Of course! And good night to ye Lady MacLeod and Duncan."

Looking back at Duncan on this, I realized from his face that he likely needed a moment to relieve himself of a night of drink before the ride home. I said, "Meet me and Angus out front."

I walked outside and told Angus that we were going to have to get Duncan and his horse back.

"All is well?"

"Thank ye cousin, all is well."

I rode on the back of Shadow as the men waked together in front to guide the horses over the rocky and uneven trail between the tavern and the castle. We remained in relative silence until they left me in the courtyard. They set about tending to the horses and, I suspect, to continue their side conversation about the evening.

"Good night, *Lady... MacLeod!*" they said in unison, mocking me.

"Good night, my trusted *knights of the realm!*"

They laughed heartily at their new, and long overdue, designation. They were and have always been my trusted knights. With Will, these men were a force for me, and I loved them.

I walked into my room and shut the door behind me, knowing that I could sleep soundly now that I had made things right with Duncan. He is the last of the council of brothers. The last father I will have in this life. And I love him with all of my heart. We have more to settle, but I feel settled this night. We have left each other on good terms.

I undressed quietly and slipped into bed to wrap my arm around the man I love more than anything in this world. I did not want to wake him, but I did want him to know that I returned home safe and sound.

"How are ye and Duncan?" Will asked quietly as he turned us both so he could wrap his strong and loving arms around me instead.

"I think we are settled. Fer now." And we were. We were settled for now.

FOURTEEN
When It All Falls Down

My husband came for me in my chamber and without a word passed Angus standing guard outside the door, and took my hand.

"Come with me!" he said. Leading me down the stairs, through the hall, and out into the courtyard, he said nothing else . I was confused as his pace increased once we were outside.

"*Will*, slow yerself!" I finally yelled, trying to wrench my hand from his and stop him from walking me across the courtyard by force. "Even though it is dark, I *cannae* have members of the clan see my own husband forcibly dragging me across the castle grounds."

"This is important, love," he said with a sense of urgency, but he slowed his walk at the same time, understanding how we could appear to anyone watching us. He placed his hand on my back instead and guided me to our destination.

We arrived at Master Morrison's surgery and he opened the door for me. Grant was laid out on a table being treated by the healer and he was a fright. His face was bloodied and brutally beaten. The man was crying out to Morrison as he tried to help set what was a severely broken left wrist which was at an ungodly and unnatural angle. His fingers were prone, and he was in severe pain for it.

"Och, dear God! Grant!" I yelled as I ran into the room to him to take his other hand in comfort and support. I kissed it over and over as he writhed in pain. "What happened!?"

The healer said softly, as he tried to tend the man's wounds, "He was beaten by men that discovered the truth of him, my lady."

My heart understood what his words meant, and I unfortunately knew in that moment this would not be the end of it.

"Did ye ken the men who did this, Grant?" I asked, wanting to know who we were dealing with. I also wanted to know if I could settle it as Lady MacLeod... because I would.

"No. I didna see a face or a voice I recognized because it all happened so fast, and it was already dark. They attacked me from behind and I got only a blurred look at the ground and then many incoming fists to my face. I passed out on the breaking of my wrist. I think someone stomped on it. I have never felt a pain like...*och, Christ!*"

"Perhaps more than once," Master Morrison said over him.

I thought for a moment of my own beating on the stone floor of MacLeod House on Canongate and know how it feels to lose your wits between the blows and tears in the moment. I breathed in deeply and in sympathy for my friend. Will saw immediately that I was also remembering my own trauma and put his hand against my back lovingly for support.

Master Morrison spoke again and said, "He was attacked in the forge and Will heard it in the stables and came to help him."

I was so proud that Will tried to help our friend and ushered me here straight away. I asked him the same question, "Will, did ye see anyone ye recognized?"

"No. I heard it happen and by the time I came around from the back into the forge, the lads had left from the front. Our paths didna cross. But from the sounds and the little I saw, I can tell ye that there was definitely more than one man involved. I can assure ye of that, my lady! More than one ran from the front of the forge."

"Did they threaten ye, Grant?" I asked, but I knew the answer as they have done more than threaten him. They have beaten the man senseless and crushed his wrist. "I mean, did they threaten *further* harm to ye?"

Grant pulled me down by my arm and said in a whisper into my ear, *"They are bringing it to ye, my lady."* He issued his warning and then, as I sat up and looked at him with tears in my eyes, he said to me again, "Aye, they are bringing it to ye in the Great Hall. That is what one man said."

I ignored this point for a moment and asked Master Morrison calmly, "Does anything here trouble ye about his injuries, sir?"

"No, my lady. He will be in pain for a few days, but it is mostly cuts and bruises. The exception being his wrist, but if I can set it right now, he should be fine."

"I hope ye are right, Cal," Grant said to Morrison, wincing in pain as he continued trying to set his wrist, "or my future working in the forge is over."

I smiled at him briefly and Morrison paused to take my hand and said, "But like ye already asked, my lady, they could harm him beyond this. Even without vocal threats, they could harm—or kill—*us both*!"

I nodded to Morrison, and I knew what must be done, even though it would break my heart. I *had* to protect them. I cannot protect them here. Grant has no future in the forge at Dunmara, broken wrist or not. And my healer will have to leave with him.

+++

We left Callum and Grant in the surgery as the patient finally fell asleep after the setting of his wrist. It was painful for him, and he could not take much more pain. He fainted many times, but thankfully, Morrison finally gave him a strong draft to lull him to sleep so he could work without the man recoiling in pain with every step and slowing his tedious work.

Once we were back in the confines of our bedchamber, I put my head on Will's shoulder and sobbed as I held on to him. My heart was broken. Will said nothing to me but held me tight. He let me express the pain and emotion that I could not show Grant in the surgery. I needed a moment to recover from my own emotions of what we just witnessed together.

"Will, ye ken he is the first friend I ever had in my life, and I was sad every summer he left me only to be happy again when he would return.

To have him leave again breaks my heart and fer this reason even more so, because he *cannae come back*!"

"My love. Grant and Morrison *cannae* stay. This beating proves that plain and simple. It was a warning, and the men could be killed."

"I ken yer right, but it is still painful. It hurts me that they have to deal with this and I cannae protect them. I cannae hear this in the Great Hall. I willna hear this charge against them! They have to go, and I need ye to help them leave us." Will just looked at me as I said to him as the tears streamed down my face. "I need ye to help them leave MacLeod lands."

"Aye," he said, kissing my cheek as he knew that my ask was as his lady, not just his wife and love.

"Find them, wake them, and put them on a horse to Glasgow," I said. "I will not have to hear this in the Great Hall if there is no one here to answer to the charge."

I took his face in my hands and said with tears in my eyes, "Will, I have to speak with Grant before he leaves. I cannae let him leave me for the last time without saying goodbye. I cannae pull Munro and ye cannae take Thunder, or someone may discover that we left the castle."

"It is a risk leaving castle grounds even without our horses, Alex. But I might be able to pull Morrison's without detection in the middle of the night."

I know Will is right, but I ignored his warning. "Get him on his horse. He can leave on it whenever he wants, because he can tell the guards that he is tending to someone on the clan lands. Then ye can help Grant."

"How, love?"

"Erm, ye can make yer way from an old passage behind the bakehouse and through the old dungeons. Follow the hall fer a bit and ye will find a small wooden door to the left that puts ye outside the castle walls on a verra narrow path. But be careful! Watch the cliff edge on the left side. It is a steep drop."

"Really?"

"Aye, we were always told this was an escape route should the castle be attacked. So, this is our escape route this night."

"Aye. I understand"

"When ye join Morrison, put Grant on his horse and tell them to meet us about a mile or so away from the castle and try not to be seen. I will follow behind ye in about an hour to give ye some room. I will meet ye outside the gates, following the same path."

Will nodded and left the room as I cried, thinking about the young lad that I have loved my entire life, and I had to tell him as much before he left me and Dunmara for the last time.

+++

Will waited for me outside the gates as I asked and guided me to the edge of the clan lands by the worn path and fortunate bright moonlight. I could not have hoped for better weather for our clandestine mission. Master Morrison and Grant were waiting for us, as we asked, about a mile from the castle grounds. Will helped me upon the ledge so that I could stand before both men.

"My lady," a weary and sleepy Grant said as he came to me and hugged me tight.

"My friend," I said, hugging him and then pulling back so I could look him in the eyes. Even with the cuts and bruises, I could see the beautiful eyes of my friend. Eyes I have loved since I was six years old.

Clearly in the physical and emotional pain from his ordeal and slowed by the remaining draft Morrison gave him, Grant said wearily, "I am so verra sorry that ye have to deal with this, Alex. I never meant to bring this to ye and worry about it being heard in the Great Hall, even if we are not here."

"Stop worrying about me," I said, stroking his face. "We want ye *to* be *safe*. And ye ken verra well, sir, I can handle myself!"

"Aye, that ye can!" Grant said with a smile as he went to shake William's hand respectfully as a gentleman and as old friends. Then he returned to me and took my hand in his.

"My lady, I told ye many times that I wasna the love ye deserved. I hoped ye would find it and ye have with Will. I wish ye nothing but happiness. I want ye to ken that I always felt like *I didna deserve yer love*. But, my friend, I have *always* felt it. I feel it tonight and I thank ye fer it."

"This is not the place for ye now. But ye are my dearest friend and I need ye both to get to Glasgow safely."

Grant just bowed his head and kissed my hand.

"We will write to each other and ye will tell me how ye both are." Knowing he has never been good at responding to letters, I was almost begging Grant to stay connected to me and trying to find some humor at the moment. "That means, sir, that I expect ye to find a quill in the city."

He just laughed with me at the thought. I stepped away from him and said to Master Morrison, "Along with his newfound quill, I expect ye to help my friend find some ink and parchment, sir."

"Aye, my lady," he said, laughing as he walked to me. "I never kent that ye understood, but I thank ye." I smiled at him as I did not have the words for him. I knew what he meant, but I could only focus on my friend.

"Ye have to go," I said to Grant as my eyes welled with tears.

He kissed my cheek and said, "I will love ye forever."

"Aye, friend! I will love ye forever."

Will and Master Morrison helped a weary and injured Grant mount his horse in the night and then led the horse over the terrain. I watched them leave us and all I could do was turn to my husband and sob into his chest at the loss of my friend and my inability to protect him on our lands. It hurt me to watch both men disappear into the dark of night.

Holding me tight in his arms, Will comforted me as I cried. My first responsibility was supposed to be about protecting those on our lands, and I failed my oldest and dearest friend. I failed as Lady MacLeod on this task. I did not admit the words to Will, but that is what I carried with us as he led me back to the castle, hand-in-hand and in silence along the rocky and narrow path.

+++

I sat across from Duncan and Auld Knox in prep for the next Great Hall. I knew what was coming for me and waited for Auld Knox to say the words. Surely he knew what happened in the forge and of the complaint being brought to me.

"We have one more item to discuss. The matter is being brought before ye, my lady, in the Great Hall by Roderick MacLeod. He is a crofter who lives close to the castle, as ye ken."

"Aye, I ken who he is. Will and I helped him with his new ewes during the lambing season."

I could tell that Auld Knox was uncomfortable saying the words, as he finally said, "His complaint...is... erm, that Grant MacAskill, an apprentice in the forge, is a *Sodomite.*"

Auld Knox almost whispered the last. He was so uncomfortable with the words he had to deliver and perhaps knowing that Grant was an old friend.

Finally completing his awkward task, he said, "I believe he wants ye to shame and banish the man from clan lands, my lady."

I did not know the man well, but he is responsible for one of the largest allocations of sheep on our lands. He is close to our age and took over the responsibility for his croft when his father died a few years ago. Ironically, Will and I helped the man through the lambing in the Spring. I am suddenly regretting offering that assistance to a man that would be so cruel and hateful.

I turned and asked Duncan, assuming he still had the pulse of the rumors on our lands, "Ye ken, what happened to Grant?"

"Aye, I heard. Did ye ken about him, lass?"

"Aye. He has been my friend since I was six years old, and I kept trying to convince him to love me over the years... and he couldna."

"I had no idea," he said, thinking about my words. "Is Grant the reason ye said ye would never marry, lass?"

I just looked at him and he immediately knew the answer to his question. He asked nothing more of me about that topic. Auld Knox sat up in his chair and said nothing to either of us. He may have been shocked by the openness of our conversation, but he should not be. He knows that Duncan and I speak to each other in an open way. He also needs to be open in this chamber himself for our new council of three to work.

"A group of men beat Grant severely and broke his wrist in an attack at the forge. Now, they are going to bring the truth of Grant and Morrison to the Great Hall."

"Morrison? The healer?" Duncan asked, seemingly surprised by the pair. Apparently, my primary source of gossip on our clan lands missed an important detail in this particular story.

"Aye, they love each other," I said, looking at him until he nodded finally in understanding. "Ye ken that I loved Grant and always will, uncle. I may not understand it all, but I want him to have the same love and support I do. Ye told me once that *we all deserve love*, and I have come to believe in the truth of yer words."

Duncan nodded to me in remembrance of his words, even if he was unsure about his own feelings about Grant and Callum as a pair. We *all* deserve love. *We all deserve love.*

"Grant was the first love I ever felt for someone not of my own family. Will and I escorted him and Morrison off our lands last night and sent them to Glasgow, because I will not hear this in the Great Hall. I *will not hear* this hateful complaint!"

"Och, my lady," Duncan said, encouraging me softly, and providing the counsel and honesty I asked him for. "The complaint brought to ye as chief *must* be heard. Ye cannae choose what complaints ye hear from kinsmen."

"Aye, but *I dinnae have* to say a word against Grant or Callum if they are not present."

"That may be true, but what does Will say about all of this?"

"Will understands but doesna at the same time. Grant has been a point of pain and jealousy for him because he kens Grant was my first love. Will is so jealous of some of the men around me. But he let me lead here, as he should as his lady, not just his wife."

Duncan just nodded his head in understanding.

"I cannae let them kill these men, and that is what they want to do, eventually. Ye ken that, Duncan! I had to send them to safety! I had to protect them the best I could as Lady MacLeod, even if that meant sending them away from the castle. It breaks my heart that I couldna defend them here on our own lands."

"Aye ye did, my lady. I support yer decision."

"Sir, I have no idea what is coming fer us in the Great Hall, but I need ye to help me. I fear I may become emotional about what this man says in front of the room. I ken that I cannae do that in the Great Hall. I think I can handle on my own, but if we need a moment to talk, please touch my back, or give me a look... give me something."

"I will follow yer lead. I will touch yer back if we need to talk, or I may speak and question the man on my own. Grant has proven to be an honorable lad. I will support ye both."

"Och, please Duncan, do that if I need a moment to collect myself or I am not asking what I should in the moment. Thank ye!"

Duncan's words touched me. Like Will, he likely did not fully understand what Callum and Grant had together, but he did not argue against protecting them or my decision to help them leave in the dark of night. For that, I respected him even more.

+++

Great Hall of Castle Dunmara–26 June 1767

- **Welcome & Appreciation:** *Lady MacLeod will show her appreciation to the lads and lasses for the summer and our hope for a new future.*
- **Announcement:** *School ended for the Summer, Friday, 5 June. Master Harmon returned to England. School will resume 17 August.*
- **Grievance:** *Roderick MacLeod has requested audience to bring a matter to the attention of Lady MacLeod.*

Seated in my chair with Duncan standing next to me in the Great Hall I called Roderick MacLeod forward. He stood before me and the entire room to speak of the *ungodly truth* of Grant MacAskill. His aberration was a stain upon this clan and the man should be made to account for his immoral behavior. It was a hate-filled and ugly speech before the clan, but one that seemed to have considerable support among many in the room. I believe the shame in the grievance was even more important to this man than the physical pain inflicted on my friend. With every word said, my pain was eased by knowing we were right to send the men away. They would *not* be safe here. They could *not* be safe here.

As I watched the man speak before me and the room, I could not help but notice the cuts and bruises on his own hand. They were clearly evident. Roderick MacLeod was involved in the attack on my friend, and I was incensed that he had the audacity to speak before me and this assembly, knowing what he—and others under his direction—had done to Grant.

"I ask that Grant MacAskill please step forward to answer the charge brought before me," I said loudly to the room.

Once I called Grant's name and he did not show himself before me or this audience, I declared that no one was there to answer the charges before us. Therefore, I had no action to take as Lady MacLeod. I fully prepared for someone who knew that Grant and I were friends to accuse me of helping him leave our lands or hiding him, but no one dared. Even Roderick did not dare, though there was something in his eyes that told me he wanted to. He was clearly disappointed with this outcome.

I should have let it go, but instead said, "Master Roderick, yer hand looks injured. We should have the healer help ye mend it before ye leave us in this room."

"Och, no, my..." the man stated to say.

I interrupted him and called out, channeling all the drama I could from my dearest friend, "Is Master Morrison here in the Great Hall? Master Morrison, we have need of yer service, sir!"

I asked loudly to the room with no response. No response was expected, of course. "I am verra sorry that we have no healer here for ye, sir."

"No, my lady. Please! Ye are verra kind to ask, but my hand is just fine."

"It looks like ye have been in a fight to have such a bruised and bloodied hand. Having no healer here, is there anything I or my uncle can do to help ye, then?" I asked, looking at Duncan and back at the man.

"No, my lady. I thank ye."

He knew exactly what I was accusing him of before everyone in the Great Hall, and he suddenly had nothing more to say. Now putting his hands behind his back to hide his swollen and cut knuckles, he retreated into the crowd along with some of his accomplices. He knew that his complaint would not bring about the pain and embarrassment on Grant that he hoped. I smiled at the thought that part of his plan had been thwarted before everyone in this room. Sadly, without having to declare it, he sadly got his wish to banish Grant from our lands.

"Before we leave this Great Hall, I want to be clear about one thing. As Lady MacLeod, I am here to serve *all* on our clan lands. Yer my *kinsman*. Yer my *family*. But *only I represent justice* on our lands and do not take kindly to others deciding to bring about justice or retribution on their own. And I most certainly dinnae appreciate being *lied to* in this forum."

The man said nothing and just stared at me, wide-eyed at the insinuation. He knew that my scolding was not just for him, it was a warning for the entire clan. I have no patience for lies before me—on any topic. I stood up and Duncan followed me out of the Great Hall and back to my chamber.

+++

"Ye took a risk asking Roderick about his hand and what ye said about lies, lass."

"I ken Duncan, but it was so hard fer me when I saw his hand. I kent that he was not just bringing the complaint on Grant before me, but he was one of the men who beat my friend. I couldna stand it! I am not ignorant, nor am I blind! And I willna be *lied* to!"

"I will say that ye made yer point, my lady! But remember," he started to say before I cut him off.

"Aye sir! Ye and Laird Graham told me all about men with thwarted ambitions *and* wounded pride."

"Exactly! Yer point was needed as a warning not just to Roderick but the entire clan, but I must tell ye to watch this man. I will do the same fer ye. His behavior tells me that he could be a problem for ye in the future. He has a lot of power in his location closest to the castle and his number of sheep."

"Aye! I thank ye, sir!"

"Fer now, perhaps our security plan has another benefit should he wish to retaliate."

"Are ye saying that I might have to deal with another threat? Not just Calder?"

"Aye, he could be another threat."

"That is unsettling. Well, this unfortunate event has left us short a hand in the forge, and no healer."

"What can ye do, my lady? And how can I help?"

"I can ask Auld John if he can make it through the summer without an apprentice or if he has someone he can advance to Grant's spot. If so, we are fine. If not, I could also ask if he had any lads that were on the path at the forge that got pulled for the shearing, knowing that we are already short on that need. I will make an exception to return a lad to the forge if he requires it."

"I expect John will probably be fine fer the summer. I can talk to him fer ye. He is a good man and willna mind taking on extra work... fer extra pay, of course."

"Of course! Thank ye! Fer the healer, I might send word to Sir Alexander Dick. Ye ken he was president of the Royal College of Physicians. He may be able to direct our request... if we can convince someone to take an assignment on remote Skye, that is."

"Aye! Well done! I like yer thinking, my lady!"

+++

FIFTEEN
Old Friends And Lost Loves

Dunmara Castle
Isle of Skye, Scotland
July 1767

We met the black carriage in the courtyard, and I was so glad to see my old friends. The ever gallant and dashing Master Campbell Forbes stepped out of the carriage first and then helped his wife, Elizabeth, down the two rickety steps.

Elizabeth was clearly with child and as happy as I was to see her, I knew that the pain of my last loss was still too fresh. Will, knowing immediately what I was thinking, put his hand behind me to stroke my back before calmly pushing me forward. I walked to the carriage to welcome them both, as I should.

"Och, my dear friends! I welcome ye both Castle Dunmara on Skye."

I shook Master Forbes' hand first and said, "It is good to see ye again, sir! And I am verra happy for ye to be here to see the clan lands ye support at such an important time."

"Lady MacLeod, it is my honor. I can see in your face that being home has been good for you."

"Elizabeth," I said, turning from him immediately and hugging my friend tight, "my congratulations to ye both, and I am so happy to have ye here on our lands."

"Alexandra," she said, looking at me with a tear in her eye, "I am so glad to see ye! I have missed ye so! This place is just stunning!"

Will and Duncan shook hands with Master Forbes. Master Knox helped guide the stable hands on the management of the carriage. Missus Gerrard helped guide the lads and lasses on the transport of their trunks and bags to the beautiful guest chamber we set for them.

I took Elizabeth's arm and said, "Come with me, my friend!"

"I am all yours!"

We walked through the Great Hall, and I led Elizabeth to my chamber where Missus Gerrard had small cakes and cheese waiting for us.

"I have missed ye so, Elizabeth."

"Aye," she said, resting herself in the first chair, clearly weary from her travels in the carriage and wrapping her hands around her swollen belly. "I have missed ye, Alexandra! When ye told me that ye didna have many women friends and it was then I realized that I didna either. My heart broke when ye left us in Edinburgh. Poor Campbell had to deal with my tears on the topic more than once."

I smiled at her and asked, "How are ye feeling, friend?"

"I am tired every day, and this bairn wants everything I have," she said with a sound of wearisome sorrow. She tried to correct herself, saying, "I am supposed to be happy, and I *am*! But if I am honest with ye as a woman, this is most difficult. It is harder than I ever imagined and want to yell at my own mother for not telling me what to expect."

"I ken... it wears on both yer emotions and yer body," I said, laughing with her. I never carried for long, so I could not fully understand what she was feeling in any way. I could only try to support her as a woman and friend.

"Exactly! But... I admit I am also scared. My feelings of happiness and contentment are laced with fear every day."

I thought about the losses I have had and the pain I felt on each of them, and the fear that a bairn could end in a moment or that ye carry the child and then die in childbirth is a fear all women must face. There is such power in carrying life, but when it leaves you, it crushes every bit of strength you ever thought you had.

"Och, Elizabeth," I said, taking her hand in mine. Elizabeth is feeling everything I felt before, but the fear of childbirth is new, because I never got that close. "Is Campbell a support to ye?"

"Aye, he is a loving and kind husband, but he *did not* want me to join him on this trip! He is still angry with me about it. We accepted your letter months ago and as the dates approached, I think he decided it would be better for me to be safe at home, perched upon plush cushions in the parlor, and under the care of his staff. But I could not! I wanted to see ye all again. I wanted to see *ye* again."

"I am so happy ye are here, but I would not approve of ye putting yerself or yer bairn at risk for such a trip across Scotland. I have made that journey twice now and cannae imagine making the trip with child as ye are, carriage or no!"

She just shook her head at me, and I took it to be her continued rebuke of our instructions. She made her decision and wanted nothing more than to be here. As a woman, I had to respect her own sense of belligerent independence.

Elizabeth went silent for a bit and then finally asked, "I am sorry, Alexandra. Is that Master Ramsay's portrait just there?"

She stood up and walked to look closer at the unfinished portrait of my father hanging on the wall across from my desk. Laird Graham told me that I could choose where this portrait hung. I decided when I became chief that his place was here with me in this chamber. He was to support me and watch over me, as any father should.

"Aye, that is the portrait they presented to us at the Advocate Society. I forgot that ye didna see it! Duncan and I could not get over the likeness and I admit, sometimes I look to my father for strength. Master Ramsay told us that his unfinished painting represented an unfinished life."

She said nothing. I worried for a moment that I had not explained the painting and its location well enough. Then she started crying. I went to her and held her while she sobbed with her head in her own hands.

"Ye loved him?" I asked in a whisper.

When she could finally speak, she said through her tears, "Aye, and I believe *he loved me.* I..." She had to catch her breath, and I took her hand in mine as we looked at my father staring back at us both. "I believe he would have asked me to marry him when he returned from Skye, but he didna have the chance. *He didna have the chance!*"

"Och, Elizabeth," I said, holding her tight as she cried, and I tried to hold my own tears to myself, but it was difficult. I love this woman, and I know that she loves me and my father. "I knew, but I didna. I couldna ask ye, but somehow, *I knew*. The way ye embraced me and the way ye talked of him... *I knew*."

She pulled back from me and, wiping her own tears, said as she held me by my arms, "Sometimes, I feel like I betrayed Alexander because I married his dearest friend. Seeing his eyes on me now breaks my heart even more."

"Ye cannae think such a thing! My father would want ye to be happy!"

"Aye, I know that. I do! But I feel like I am a traitor at the same time."

"Elizabeth, my father is gone from this life and ye are betraying nothing. He can no longer be the love ye seek." I could not imagine what she was feeling, and I could see that while she was happy, she still carried a broken heart. In fact, her broken heart may have brought her all the way to Skye. She needed to see Alexander's home, even at the risk of her child or her own life.

I wanted to share more with her. I wanted to ask her more about my father, but I could not say the words now. We had too many emotions and revelations in one afternoon, and I could tell that she was growing weary.

"Surely the men are done with their management of carriages and horses. Let me take ye to yer bedchamber. I hope ye will find it fine. Ye

194

need to rest before supper and in fact, yer husband may already be there waiting and wondering where ye are."

"Aye," she said with a smile as she wiped her tears and went with me toward the door, "and it takes me longer these days to get myself together."

We walked together arm-in-arm and Master Forbes was indeed at the door directing the young lads on the placement of chests, and some were bringing in new cauldrons of water to place by the fire.

"I will leave ye here. Take yer rest and William and I will collect ye both at six o'clock to escort ye to the head table. The entire clan is anticipating the great food, music, and drink fer ye this night. Prepare yerselves! Ye may be asked to dance!"

They both smiled at me as I said gripping Elizabeth's hand in mine, "I leave ye here in the company of yer husband and thank ye, sir, for allowing me time with my dear friend today. Please let me or Missus Gerrard know if ye need anything."

"Elizabeth has missed you dearly, Alexandra," he said, taking her hand from mine and escorting her into their room. I nodded to him in understanding and walked away. I missed her very much as well.

+++

"Och, Will," I said into his ear as he kissed my cheek before we went to retrieve our guests.

I looked into his eyes, and he could see my sorrow as he said softly, *"I ken, my love."*

"I wanted nothing more than to have the only woman friend I have ever had here, and I am happy she is, but I am jealous of her at the same time. Does that make me a horrible person?"

"Everything happens as it should. Dinnae be heartbroken on yer own loss, but be happy for the life yer friend has within her... one ye hope she carries all the way safely and that she and the bairn are healthy."

"Aye, yer right. Master Garrick said I have to focus on the *hope*."

"Aye, choose *hope* today—fer ye and yer friend."

"Upon seeing the Ramsay portrait fer the first time in my chamber, Elizabeth confessed to me time that she loved my father, and he loved her."

"Yer intuition was right all along on that score, then!"

"Aye," I said, looking at my shoes. "I love her all the more that father loved her. I know that sounds strange as I say the words aloud, but there is something to be said that we were both drawn to her. It tells me that she is a genuine person."

"I understand that lass, because I believe she loves ye both the same." I looked at him with a confused look and furrowed brow as he said, slightly correcting his thought. "I ken it is *not* the same, but ye look like Alexander, and ye represent him in a way that is not a memory or a painting. Yer the closest she will ever get to seeing him in this life again."

I kissed him and said, "Och, my darlin' man, that is absolutely right! I had not thought of it that way. What a lovely thought!"

+++

Will and I met Campbell and Elizabeth, in all of our fine clothes, outside their bedchamber. We all walked together downstairs to the head table where our guests had seats of honor between us and Duncan.

I stood, taking my glass in hand, and said to the room as I raised it, "Tonight, Clan MacLeod, we welcome our dear friends and our advocate here to Castle Dunmara. We welcome Master Campbell Forbes and his wife, Missus Elizabeth. I say to ye all as we enjoy the bounty of this hearty supper and drink that may be never-ending. *Slainte mhath!*"

"*Slainte mhath!*" the room said in agreement.

We all ate in celebration for our new guests and Missus Gerrard prepared a fine feast for the occasion. We ate and drank well into the evening. The men began talking amongst themselves at the end of the table.

"Alexandra, are ye happy in yer marriage?" Elizabeth asked me directly at some point.

I tried not to sound defensive, but I was shocked by the question but answered her right away, "Of course I am! Why do ye ask me that?"

She just looked at Will and then me and said, "Ye seem... erm, sad."

I could barely breathe that she could see what had been months of torment and said, "Och, my friend."

She could see the tears forming in my eyes and said like she did in Edinburgh, "Look at me, *look at me.*"

When I did, the tears immediately retreated. I asked loudly as I stood and took her hand, "Elizabeth, should we leave the men to have their whisky and talk together again in my chamber?"

She smiled and said, rubbing her belly, "Aye, thank ye, Lady MacLeod. Perhaps we can walk a bit together first."

"Will, I look to ye and Duncan to host our dear friend Campbell fer a moment."

"Aye, the ladies should have their time to talk," Will said as he kissed me on the cheek.

Elizabeth and I walked together a bit around the room before retreating to my chamber. Once Elizabeth was seated opposite me in front of the desk, she asked me, "What is wrong, friend?"

"Och," I said as I tried to keep my tears behind my eyes. "Since leaving the city, I have had a difficult time."

She just looked at me and nodded her head. I had not talked fully of what happened, but she could imagine with the truth of what happened and the continued search for Calder.

"I am haunted by what happened at MacLeod House and the ghost of him, for sure. He continues to torment me. While I ken that I am loved by my husband and my family, I also ken that sometimes it was not enough to keep the sadness and pain from me."

"And bairns, lass?"

Her question, as my friend, was fair. She just shocked me. I have not had to declare fully to anyone else outside my family. I looked at her and said the truth of it.

"Aye, since the attack in Edinburgh, I have lost one more."

"Och, my darling," she said, with her tears now falling on her cheeks for me. She did not say the words, but I am certain she thought about what sitting before me swollen with child may make me feel and I would never tell her anything other than she has brought me hope. Hope for a new life and that one day I can be where she is now. But also hope that she and her bairn are safe when they return home. Will was right to remind me of this, and I *do* believe it.

"Will is my love and tries so hard to bring me nothing but comfort, but I fear Calder harmed me more than we can understand. I worry that he is not dead—as we all hope—and I will see him at any moment."

I stood up and looked out of the window to the sea I love and said, "I live in that fear every day, as his shadow lurks around every corner and in every crowd... even here in the comfort of home."

I had always carried the ghost of Calder, but what should be a place of comfort had been shattered. I could not tell Elizabeth of the ominous message delivered in the village not long ago, that we believe he is on Skye, or that the trail on the man has gone cold once again. Not knowing where he is means he remains a fearful specter... a threat.

I turned to see my friend looking at me with a worried look. She did not ask me any questions. I continued my confession, "I returned to Skye broken."

"*Alexandra,*" she said softly, looking down at the sorrow of my words.

"No, I was! I didna want anyone else to think it, but *I was broken*. And I hurt myself in every way I possibly could."

She looked up at me in an instant curious and concerned as to what I could mean by such words.

"I stopped eating, and I cut myself on my arms just here," I said, lifting my sleeve to show the remnant scars of abuse and pain that I carried on the outside to represent and honor those that I carried on the inside.

"Why would ye do such a thing, lass?" she asked, taking my hand forcibly and with a pained look tenderly touched the raised scars on my arm herself.

"I told everyone that if I hurt myself, I didna have to think about anyone else hurting me. It was an act of controlling something that I couldna control otherwise. I was trying my best to control... my own *fear. My own emotions.*"

Holding my hand tighter now, she said, "I dinna mean to diminish anything ye have had to endure, Alexandra, and I cannae say I understand it all, but ye are the strongest woman I know. Ye are young, not even married a year, and ye will keep trying."

"That is exactly what Will says," I said, trying to smile back at her through my own tears. I laughed as I said, "And he does like to try."

"They *all* like to try, my friend. But it is all a miracle and will happen when it is supposed to."

I just nodded at her words because they were true. I needed to remember that it was a miracle.

"I hope Master MacCrimmon is a comfort to ye. I can see that he is still trying to get your attention. The man never takes his eyes off ye. *Never!*"

"Och, friend! He is good to me and a good partner here at the castle. But I admit that we have had some struggles. Some as a result of my own torments from Edinburgh and some from just getting used to being married. I am fiercely independent, and Will is so jealous of other men. I swear to God! I bet the man even watches Father Bruce like a hawk!"

Laughing, Elizabeth said, "I bet he does! Ye ken every man has such insecurities where his wife is concerned. Ye should be worried if he *stops* being jealous."

"Is Campbell the same?"

"Aye, the man has replaced some of the men on his staff at the house with women to care for me. He kept his own valet, of course, but the man is under strict orders not to be in a room alone with me."

"No!" I said in disbelief that he would be so protective.

"It is true. Of course, it is most humorous because I am fairly certain the man is not particularly fond of women in general. But Campbell cannae see it. All he sees is an imaginary threat that he must prevent."

"Men are curious creatures, are they not?"

"Aye, but we love them anyway."

"That we do."

"I am so glad ye and Campbell are here! I will escort ye back to yer bedchamber and hope ye will join us on the tour of Glenammon tomorrow."

"Aye, I cannae wait to see what Master MacLeod has built!"

+++

SIXTEEN
Reclaiming The Future

Campbell joined me, Will, and Duncan in my chamber before we left for the tour of the newly built Glenammon on Skye.

"I have the contracts for you to sign, Alexandra," Campbell said, pulling the parchment from his bag.

"It makes me so pleased, Campbell, that ye and Elizabeth will live at the house on Canongate," I said, opening the ink well on my desk and dipping in the quill.

"Aye, Elizabeth is most happy with the purchase," he said as we signed the papers together. "You were so generous in offering the house for our wedding and we both had family stay there, so got to see more of it and decided it was perfect for us and our new family. Much more suitable than my small set of rooms near my office and with the bairn on the way so soon. This is best for us for... now."

"I suspect that copper bath was a positive selling point," I said, smiling at him as I signed where he told me to on each page of the contract.

"How could it not be?" he said, smiling back at me. "The detailed inventory you and Master MacCrimmon prepared helped me also see that the house was undervalued, so I have placed £5,200 pounds sterling into your account."

"I told ye I expected ye to pay a handsome price, sir," I said, shaking his hand at the completion of our business.

"You did, indeed! I could not in good conscience pay an unfair price to you for the property. And true to Alexander's wishes, we will keep Missus Douglas and Master Harris employed in our service, so from this point, their wages will no longer come from your account."

"I thank ye, sir," I said, smiling at the thought that no one would be displaced from their home or work—just as father wanted.

"I believe Missus Douglas and Elizabeth have grown quite fond of each other in this short time."

"No doubt due to Missus Douglas' wonders in the kitchen and sweet wee Petey's work on the steps."

"We may be short on our stay, as I have already started the process of contracting a property in New Town, but I believe the building will sell and I can bring the contents of the house to our new home on Charlotte Square. I have contracted the lot your father wished to buy, as the one I was looking at further up Princes Street was suited more for a bachelor than a family."

I smiled at him and the thought of him and Elizabeth having the house they deserve. But part of me regretted Father's loss of not moving to a home that he wanted or being happy with his own love there.

"But I commit to you now, we are making certain that we have room so that we can have Master Harris and Missus Douglas and Petey join us at the new house. They will retain their positions and have their own accommodations just as they do today."

"Och, I appreciate that so much, sir! Thank ye! Truly!"

"And no offers fer Glenammon House?" William asked.

"None yet, but I have not given up," Campbell said back to him. "It is a fine property but would say again that with the inventory the price should be close to what Canongate sold for. The building and contents, land, boathouse, and stables are grand for such a house. Almost even more so than the house in the city."

Thinking ahead to what we might discuss at Glenammon Brewery and Distillery on the west side of the country, I said, "It may work to our advantage that the house has *not* sold. We will ride out to see what Duncan has accomplished here on Skye and tell ye of our thoughts for the future. With yer advice and counsel, we may decide to retain Glenammon House in MacLeod hands."

Campbell looked at me unsure of what I was saying. William, and Duncan understood that I was intent on preserving the name as much as the house.

"Then this trip will be most intriguing in many ways," Campbell said to me with a smile.

+++

Master Knox and wee Robbie had the horses and Master Forbes's carriage ready for our trip to the new Glenammon. While a short trip, Elizabeth was in no state to sit atop a horse, so I rode with her and Campbell in the carriage behind Will and Duncan.

"Duncan will take ye through his work establishing a distribution center and brewery here on the West Coast of Scotland first. Then he will share the plan for a distillery in the future. Ye ken that is his ultimate goal. We welcome your honest feedback and questions."

"Of course! Ye are both my clients and I only want ye to be successful. Your success is my success."

"This is Duncan's inheritance. His business. I will only tell ye our thinking about the future and other ways ye may help us with the brewery and beyond at the end of his tour."

He looked at me for a moment and nodded his head in agreement. He understood that I was asking to give Duncan his moment, and my uncle knew that this would be our approach. Shipping and brewery first and then the future, which we will cover together.

"Och, Alexandra!" Elizabeth said, looking out of the window as we pulled up to the new building behind the new stone wall and gates. "It is verra impressive."

"Aye," Campbell said, "it looks verra much like the brewery building in Leith, just a tad smaller."

"I am certain he was influenced by the original."

Will helped us all from the carriage and Duncan began his tour of the building and operation, including the preview of the distillery. Campbell tasted the early batch and, like us, found it a warm taste that would only become smoother and richer with age. Campbell and Elizabeth both selected the same bottle I did, and we had a laugh that, with the exception of Will, that we all had the same tastes.

Elizabeth spoke first and said, "Ye should be verra proud of what ye have done here, Master MacLeod!"

"I thank ye for the kind words, missus," Duncan said proudly. He has done a great deal of work on the building and the business. His focus has been clear and as much as I have missed him, he has made great progress in this new building. Duncan looked at me, and I knew it was time to tell the rest of the story.

"Campbell, I told ye on the carriage ride here that I am also proud of what Duncan has done, but I also wanted us to talk about the future."

He nodded to me in understanding.

"Duncan, Will and I have been thinking. Glenammon is my father's and I want us to reclaim it. That means I want to ensure that all the operations at Leith and the operations here on Skye—including the future distillery—remain in MacLeod hands."

"Ye mean to buy out Drummond, then?" Campbell asked, looking at all of us.

"Aye, we do," I said, standing between my uncle and my husband, "with yer guidance, of course. The economy of sheep, fishing, and farming will keep us alive but will not protect the clan from the changes that are already happening across our lands."

He just looked at me as I continued, "Crofters continue to leave Skye for the cities or the colonies, and I have fewer and fewer people to work in traditional roles. In fact, this summer, fewer lads came to Dunmara for the largest shearing we have ever had. So, I need to think about other forms of income, and it is evident to us all that father prospered with ale.

We believe the addition of whisky and a storage and distribution center on this side of the country only adds to the possibility of success and profit to the clan."

Master Forbes nodded his head in silent agreement as I continued, "If we can reclaim Glenammon, we can offer roles here on Skye and in the cities beyond for MacLeod kinsmen to continue to serve MacLeod interests. So, I am asking fer yer counsel on such a plan and if ye will help us negotiate with Master Drummond."

I stopped talking for a moment. Duncan nodded to me that I successfully made our case. Will silently placed his hand on my back, showing me that he also believed I represented our plan to our advocate well.

"Alexandra, you are saying *we,* but Duncan owns the majority stake in Glenammon. Will you be purchasing the brewery operations from your inheritance or will he?"

Before I could answer a question that none of us discussed, Duncan said, "Alexandra should have everything fer the clan. We didna discuss this far as a family. But I would like Alexandra to buy the brewery operations to free me completely to the distillery. Do ye agree, Alex?"

"Aye, as this will benefit the clan, I would like to purchase the name, brewery, and ale rights on both sides of the country. Duncan's leadership will be essential across both, of course, but we will work together where we need to represent the name Glenammon, but he should retain full ownership of the distillery, which is part of his inheritance. It should be fer him and his own family. But the clan will own the name and benefit from it."

Duncan nodded to me, and I realized that this was the first time that I thought of him caring for a family of his own one day, but the distillery was of his own creation. It is his.

Duncan spoke and said, "And if I never have a family of my own, I would want everything to go back to the clan. Ye can help me there, Campbell, so that my wishes are kent."

I looked at Duncan on these words with a smile. After spending so much time hoping to be alone myself, I wanted my uncle to have the hope of his own family one day. I had no hope that would be with Missus Harold, but he deserved everything I had. We waited for Campbell to say something. The silence in the room made me nervous, and I had to restrain myself. I wanted to keep talking to fill the void, as I usually do... so I did.

"I will add that I think Glenammon House not selling is a benefit to our family and our clan. If we can make this work, I want to retain the house myself because we will have to visit operations on that side of the country several times a year."

He smiled at me and said, "I think this is a good plan, but I have a question. Who will run your brewery in Leith?

We all looked at him. We had a plan but not that specific of a plan. Master Forbes called us out our lack of preparedness with his question.

"I mean no offence, but as Lady MacLeod, ye have responsibilities here on Skye that ye cannot abandon and have already declared that Duncan will focus on the distillery."

"No offence taken, sir! And ye are correct! I will ensure that we have the best people in the location at Leith. I have seen nothing that tells me based on the money that put in my account prior to Duncan taking over that they do not run a good business operation at the brewery. They do!"

"Aye!" Duncan said. "And I can confirm based on my account, they are continuing to do well."

"Aye, that is true," Campbell said.

"I would trust the oversight of the transition to no one, but our family and I would like to have Will's help if he is open to the idea."

I looked at Will only briefly as the shock on his face startled me. I had not discussed this idea with Will or Duncan, but I believe this is right. William should come out of the stables and run this for our family and our clan. I know that means he would be away from me for part of the year, which breaks my heart. He may not think that he knows the business of brewing, but he is more than capable. He will learn what he needs to, and his own intellect and honest character will handle the rest.

"I admit to ye all that this is not something we have discussed and will need to—as a family. But he is the only man I trust on this. I hope he can find a leader to run it for us or confirm that we have the right leadership already in place so that we only have to check on them at certain points during the year. Of course, Duncan and Will can depend on me as much as they need to."

"I will serve as ye command, my lady, and I am here to help my family," Will said but still uncertain as he was put on the spot in front of everyone for a responsibility he never asked for. He took my hand in his. I felt his obedience and his hurt because this means we will send him away from Skye when the deal is done.

Campbell was silent again and then smiled as he said, "I think this is a fine plan. And you all may be in luck on the ask. From what I understand, Master Drummond has been looking to sell his stake in Glenammon."

"Really?" I asked in shock, looking at everyone in the room. My eyes growing larger looking at Duncan and William. "We *must* get to him before he sells to someone else, sir!"

"Aye! I heard rumblings of this just before we left Edinburgh. Apparently Drummond likes to play the cards and has lost a good bit of his money in the process. I can try to negotiate on your behalf, and I believe the man would be more than willing to have cash on hand."

"Sir, I ken what he paid to buy out Duncan for a small portion, but I am not willing to pay more than what is fair, and I am not in any mind to cover any of Drummond's gambling debts."

"No, Lady MacLeod and I would not bring that kind of offer. You have my word on that! And I would want to look closely at their books again to ensure Drummond has not been hiding his personal debts in the ledgers in any way."

"Then that is our ask, sir. Come back to us with your assessment of current leadership at the operation and a price for the brewery operations at Leith. And fer now, I will retain Glenammon House and continue to pay the wages of Master and Missus Cameron from my account. Ye can stop trying to sell the property."

I looked at Elizabeth and she smiled at me and nodded her head. I felt good that I had done what my father asked of me. He may not have seen this future for his family. Or even if he did, the Clan MacLeod was prepared to look to the future with ale and whisky... and not just sheep and tenant rents.

Once again, we will try to lead by his example and be ahead of our time.

+++

I chose to ride back to Castle Dunmara on the back of Will's horse, leaving the carriage to just Elizabeth and Campbell alone for the short ride back to the castle.

"I apologize fer telling Campbell that I wanted Will to lead the brewery operations, without talking to ye, love or Duncan first."

Duncan spoke before Will could and said, "I would have said the same thing, my lady."

"Aye, but I ken nothing of the brewing business, and will that not take me away from ye, love?"

I had not thought through this plan but said, "Will, ye are the only one we trust, at least at the start. But this is why I kept Glenammon House, because we may have to be there for some time."

"But what about your role here?"

"The three of us are going to have to figure that part out," I said, looking at Duncan. "We might have to help each other. And we have some time before Campbell gets back to us on the negotiations with Drummond."

Duncan looked at me but said nothing. But that was the truth of it. The beginning may be difficult, and we might have to help each other as a family.

+++

Our guests were set to leave us and make the journey across Scotland back to the city. I hated to see them leave us, but wanted nothing more than to get Elizabeth and her bairn home safe.

"I am sad to see ye both leave, but I will be happy to hear ye have arrived safely home and delivered. Ye must write to me immediately, friends."

Elizabeth spoke first, saying, "I am so proud of ye, Alexandra. Ye have been such a gracious host and ye are doing what you are meant to as the lady of this clan. I told ye once that ye were a remarkable woman and everything that I have seen here tells me I was right."

She kissed me on the cheek, and I hugged her tight. "I ask it again friend, please write to me and let me know about yer bairn. I cannae wait to hear everything!"

"I will, I promise!"

Before we both got too emotional, Master Forbes said, "This trip was most beneficial to me as your advocate and friend. I heard a great deal from Alexander over the years, of course, but being here is different. I am impressed and proud to serve you all. Thank you! Thank you for hosting us the way you did and thank you for giving more insight."

He kissed the top of my hand before he shook hands with all the men. "Lady MacLeod, I did not say the words to you at the moment, but I want you to know that I think what you are doing here—reclaiming Glenammon for the clan—is *extraordinary*! Like your father, you are ahead of your time. You can see a future ahead of you that no one else can. You will hear from me soon about your plans for the future. As always, I am here to serve you and Clan MacLeod."

I looked at Duncan, who nodded to me as I said back to the man, "Aye, we look forward to yer discussions with Drummond. Thank ye sir, and I was most happy to see Elizabeth. Please be safe on yer journey home. I pray fer yer safe return to Edinburgh and wish ye only happiness for your new family, in your new home—the new Forbes House on Canongate."

Will took my hand as we stood and watched the carriage leave the gates. Much like my own departure many months ago, all I could hear were the sounds of the horses along with the wheels of the carriage on the ground and the prayers for our travelers from Father Bruce.

+++

I turned to face Will and looked at him, reading his book of sonnets. I propped my head on my hand and whispered across my pillow, "I was so happy to have Elizabeth here."

"Aye, and I am glad ye could have the support of a friend. I felt the change in ye. There is only so much comfort a man can give."

"Ye are a comfort, my love. But I agree, the comfort and guidance from a woman was much needed at this time."

"Elizabeth is one of the best things to come out of that trip to Edinburgh! I can see how happy her friendship makes ye," he said before putting his book aside and turning to kiss me.

"Will, *ye* are the best thing to come out of that journey! Elizabeth is the second best... but a close second," I said, teasing him.

"She replaced Munro, then?" he asked with a sly smile.

"Och, no! I suppose she is third on that list! Munro would *never* forgive me if I replaced him with two people! One was hard enough!"

"Ye and that blasted horse!"

"Will, ye ken..."

"I ken! I ken! *Munro is a verra special lad!*" He said, rolling his eyes and reminding me how much I love his humor and how there was absolutely no limit to the man's jealousy—even for a horse.

+++

SEVENTEEN
Prometheus Of Castle Rock

Dunmara Castle
Isle of Skye, Scotland
August 1767

My first summer leading as the Lady MacLeod was ending. It was a challenge of leadership for me throughout and one that redistributed the lads and lasses across our lands in support of the shearing.

MacLeod lands have more sheep than people at this time, and we hope the changes made for this summer benefit the clan in the long run. This includes greater production across meat, wool, and the inevitable increased rents from crofters with more heads. I stood in the courtyard talking to wee Robbie and William as we watched the last of the lads leave us when Angus tore into the courtyard on his horse.

Shadow was a monster, and this day, both of their nostrils were flared, heaving with purpose—and not just from a swift ride across our lands. They were on a mission!

Angus jumped off his horse and yelled to Will, "Where is Duncan?!"

Will said, "I dinna ken! Angus, can we help ye?"

"Where is the man!?"

I spoke up and said, "I think he is still in the hall, cousin. What is wrong?"

"Ye both need to come wi'me," he said to us and handed the reins to wee Robbie. "Robbie, lad, keep Shadow 'ere. Water the beast, but I will be back for 'im in a moment."

Robbie nodded to him. Will and I followed a manic and surprisingly clear Angus through the corridor to the Great Hall. Sure enough, there was my uncle talking to a group of men rearranging the tables for supper and Angus motioned him to join us at the side of the other side of the room.

"Are ye alright, Angus?" I asked, looking at him and then Will, trying to determine what was happening. He just looked at me but did not answer.

When Duncan joined us, he asked immediately, "What is it, man? Ye look a fright!"

He looked at all of us and then said, catching his breath from his ride and run into the hall, "I was in the Old Stone and a man came in asking about the Lady MacLeod. I was drinkin' and talkin' wi' Auld Jonah, and m'ears perked up."

His eyes grew wide with the story he had to tell. "So, I tried to engage the man to see what 'e wanted, aye? I bought 'im drinks and tried to get 'im to talk, *and 'e did!*"

Looking at me, he paused for a moment and said to Duncan, "It is Calder."

I nearly fell off my feet had my husband not caught me with his hand and lifted me back up by my skirts and kept his hand behind my back.

"I am sorry, m'lady," Angus said, reaching to help me stand with Will. I know that he did not want to hurt me. This was not unexpected. I have been waiting for the intruder to show himself for some time—in due time as he threatened—but the words still took me back.

Duncan was also concerned for me, and asked calmly, "How do ye ken this, man?"

"Like ye said, m'lady, the man doesna look the same," he said to me, shaking his head, "but 'e is just as arrogant and cold as ever. Once a chancer, always..."

I finished his standard line, "... always a chancer!"

He nodded to me, but then said to his friend, "Duncan, erm, m'lady, erm... he says he has Alexander's gold watch."

I stepped back away from them with tears in my eyes. The ghost haunting me for months since his ominous note and his tease of the gold chain delivered to me in Dunmara Village has shown himself finally. I am devastated and relieved at the same time. We all knew that he was here on Skye. I was right to be afraid of him returning, but the specter was real at this very moment. It was not just my mind reliving pain on its own. The threat has been there all along and now he is close. He is too close.

"Aye, m'lady," Angus looked at me apologetically as he said, "The man says, 'e is carryin' the watch... *and*... the pearls."

I bowed my head and started crying before my knights, as they were the only people I could cry in front of. They all moved me out of the room to my chamber at once to give me a moment to collect myself out of the view of other members of the clan. William almost carried me in his arms as I tried to catch my breath. I could not breathe through my sobs!

Once in the lady's chamber, I walked to my desk but did not make it to my chair. I started falling to the floor, shaking, and rubbing my left arm, feeling the old scars still there for strength but they could not keep me standing. Will immediately picked me up by my elbows and helped me to my chair as I tried to regain my composure.

"These are the only two items missing from the wooden box Father left me," I said to them all through my tears and nearly sick to my stomach, "and *only* the people in this verra room kent what was missing when we found the box Master Forbes told us of. *It is him!* He is no longer a ghost or a memory. *He is here!*"

I looked at Will, who nodded his head with regret that it was *him*. We all knew it was Calder and the thoughts of why and how he had these items in his possession were also racing through our minds.

Duncan was always practical, but deferring to me in my role as Lady MacLeod, took the lead and said, "What would ye would like us to do fer ye, my lady?"

I could see in his eyes with his question that Duncan was just begging me to give him permission to kill the man. Part of me wanted to order him to do it and end it for us all. But, instead, I had to hear the truth of it. We *all* needed to hear the truth of it. I ignored Duncan's question for a moment.

"Angus, is the man still at the tavern?"

"I asked Auld Jonah to keep giving the man plenty of whisky or wine on my promise of payment so that I could come 'ere and get ye. He doesna ken the reason, but I was clear that the man should stay there as long as he could, even if he 'ad to offer 'im lodging fer the night. Jonah kens I am good fer the payment and I believe Calder *kens* 'e will see ye. The man said as much."

Duncan asked his question again, "What would ye would like us to do fer ye, my lady?"

"I would like us all to go to the Old Stone and hear the confession of Allan Calder, *Esquire*," I said coldly to my uncle, Angus, and Will as my tears dried instantly on my cheeks.

None of these men could fault me for wanting to hear the truth. They wanted to hear it as well. I worried if their male pride and protectiveness would get in the way. This is the first time I could truly direct them as their lady to stand down and wait for my command before the man met his inevitable fate.

+++

I stood in our room as my husband helped me into my cloak for the trip to the Old Stone Tavern. Angus and Duncan were in charge of preparing our horses for the trip.

"Before we go, what are ye thinkin' love?" Will asked me.

"I have to hear the truth," I said. He kissed me and I said I in his ear as I hugged him tight and said, *"I need ye to support me."*

"Aye, my love, always!"

"No, Will. Fer the first time, I am asking ye to support me as Lady MacLeod, not yer wife and love."

"Aye," he said, nodding that he knew the difference in what was expected of him.

"I have to ken the truth from Calder, and ye cannae do anything to keep me from that! We will *all* want to kill him fer our own reasons when we see him in person and hear what he has to say. I told ye we would make him confess, and we will. But his confession has to be heard. All of it."

Will nodded in agreement but I could tell that he was thinking that this was going to be a true test of his resolve and restraint to not kill the man that hurt his wife and family so.

"Will, I am scared about what he will say about *how* he has these items and *what* he did to me. Ye and I are both going to want to kill him, but we cannae. I need ye to respect me for my position, sir. And I will need yer help with the others, aye?"

"Aye."

"Especially Duncan! If the man says what I suspect to be true, it will take all of us to pull him back from killing Calder—orders from Lady MacLeod or not."

"Aye, ye think he stole these items from yer father's house?"

I nodded to him. It was obvious that Calder stole the items from my father, but there was a possibility that the man killed him before doing so. I did not say the words and Will did not ask me to explain, but he understood my direction. He would help restrain Duncan if he had to.

Angus, while a battlefield warrior, would have no remorse killing the man on principle and could have before even bringing us to the tavern, but will not disobey an order, so I am less worried about him taking matters into his own hands.

We joined Angus and Duncan in the courtyard, and the four of us rode in silence. Outside the tavern door, I asked Angus, "Cousin, is the man still there and can ye tell if anyone else is in the room?"

Angus stepped inside the door and came back to us and said, "Aye, 'e is just talking to Auld Jonah. The only other in the tavern is Danny MacLean, and 'e is blind drunk with 'is 'ead already on the table."

"I have made my request to Will already, but my ask is that each of ye follow my lead as yer lady. Do ye understand? I have to hear the truth... *all* of it! Even if it *hurts* us to hear it—and it will hurt us. *Please* let me finish this!"

They all nodded to me in agreement and said in unison, *"Aye, my lady."*

"And Angus, Auld Jonah, needs to hear what is said as an independent party to this conversation. It cannae just be our family hearing this confession. He does not need to be in the middle of it, just ask him to stay close enough to hear us."

"Aye, m'lady."

Will took my hand in his for a moment in support and smiled at me. I smiled back but let his hand go so that I could lead my knights into the tavern where I sat down opposite a weather-worn and a very drunk, Allan Calder.

+++

As I took my cloak off and let it hang on the back of my chair, my three knights stood behind me. He was not as beaten, swollen, and bloodied as when I last saw him. While he looked different still, it was clear it was the man we knew. He did not have the slick, black grease in his hair or the dark clothing, but Calder revealed himself and it sent a chill down my back to see him before me.

Angus brought Auld Jonah close by way of bringing us drinks that none of us were going to touch and he remained close enough to the end of the bar to hear what was happening in his tavern. Like Angus said, Danny MacLean, who was clearly passed out, had no more need of his attention this night.

As scared as I was to see the ghost I dreaded for months before me, I said calmly and with all the confidence I could muster, "I hear ye are looking for Lady MacLeod, sir."

For a moment, I resented being so formal with my words and the use of the term 'sir' for a man that did not deserve my respect. I am sure my disdain was evident on my face. Calder's eyes lit up, and he sat up straight in his chair until he saw the men standing behind me. In the half-second of fear he felt, he wasted no time and immediately reverted back to the arrogant man he has always been.

"Aye, *Alexandra*! I see ye still have all yer *dogs* at yer service."

"Ye will address me as *Lady MacLeod*," I said to the man as coldly as I could. At least he did not call me *lass*, as he did in Father's office. But his distasteful look and disrespectful tone were very much the same—even without the use of the word.

"*Lady MacLeod*," he said, slurring his speech with considerable drink, "I have something of yers." I just looked at him, waiting for him to speak again. He started rubbing his cold, blue hands together, as he continued, "I am here to tell ye I have yer father's gold watch *and* pearls."

"And how is it that ye have these items, sir?" I said, looking around the room as I laughed, "If they *are my father's* at all!"

He leaned forward in his chair and looked at me with the same disdain he had from the beginning, and snarled at me, "I *took* them from yer father, so they *must* be his!"

I could see Duncan move forward and tilted my head slightly in his direction to remind him to follow my lead.

"When did ye take these items?"

The man took another sip of his drink, and Auld Jonah, playing his part as witness and bar keep well, refilled the glass immediately for the man. He remained on the side of the bar, out of sight but still able to hear our discussion.

"When we returned from Skye, Master MacLeod let me know that I was not of the caliber of lawyer or character that he wanted, representing his clients or his *own good name.*"

"I believe I told ye the same, Master Calder," I said as a matter of fact. I could be so bold, knowing it was the truth and knowing that I had brave men standing guard behind me, ready to protect me in an instant.

He moved toward me in anger, and all three of my knights moved to match him. He backed down and continued, "He said that I would not take any clients more in his practice, and he had written a letter to Master Forbes and the Advocate Society about his opinion. Upon his word, I would never work in the legal profession in Edinburgh again."

"If this was the case, sir. Why did my father bring ye all the way to Skye?" The men looked at me, but this was a mystery that we needed to solve. A mystery we discussed together months earlier in the White Hart Inn. *Why did my father bring someone he did not trust to Skye?*

He thought about his answer before saying, "He didna say, but I suspect he was trying to keep an eye on me before making his final decision. He didna trust to leave me in Edinburgh while he was away. However, I believe it was also to keep me from Mistress Hay. The man wanted *that* bonnie lass fer *himself*."

Just as I said before, *'keep yer enemies closer.'* I made notice that Allan Calder just added my dear friend Elizabeth to the list of things he believes the MacLeod's have taken from him. I was *incensed*.

He took a sip of his drink and kept talking, "So I found my way into the house on Canongate by an unmanned close determined to take this letter before first light. I found the letter on his desk and destroyed it in the last of the fire but realized in an instant that would *not be enough*. The man could just write another. So, I went upstairs and confronted Master MacLeod in his bedchamber."

My heart sank, and I closed my eyes. I knew what Calder was going to say, and I knew that I could not keep Duncan from him if he said the words I expected aloud—lady's orders or not.

"Fer such a grand house, Canongate is a verra easy house to get in and out of," he said arrogantly, sipping his refilled glass with a smile, "as ye ken, *Lady MacLeod*."

This time, William moved slightly forward. But these men may just have to hold me back if I decide to go for Calder first.

"Master MacLeod was still in bed and woke when I entered his bedchamber. I told him that I would not let him ruin me or my name." I almost laughed as this man has no name, no reputation, and his arrogance before me is making my blood boil. "I was so angry, but I had no choice! He started yelling, so I placed a pillow over his face to silence him until he died."

I bit my bottom lip and tried my best not to show any emotion. I did not say the words to Will, but for the man to have father's belongings meant that he had not only stolen these items, but he had likely killed my father to have them in his hands in the first place. If he had arrived after my father's death, as he originally said, he would have had Missus Douglas and Doctor Tyndall in the room with him.

Just then, Duncan lurched forward and punched Calder twice in the face as hard as he could, screaming, "I will kill ye myself, ye goddamned weasel!" It took the strength of both Will and Angus to drag him away from the man.

"*Give me yer command, my lady!*" Duncan pleaded, struggling in their grip. "*Please! Give me yer command!*"

Calder sat back up on his chair, spit a mouthful of blood and two of his jagged and already broken teeth onto the floor. The pain and anger in Duncan's eyes and voice broke my heart. Part of me wanted him to end it for all of us. I bit my lip and looked at my men, silently asking them to let me get the full story. We had at least one more sin to hear.

Duncan broke himself from the restrictive arms of Will and Angus and reluctantly returned to his station behind me. I could hear him breathing hard and seething with anger, but he remained at his post and said nothing more.

I asked calmly, "And then?"

"The box was on the table beside his bed and open, I took the watch and the pearls off the top, and then heard the auld missus coming up the stairs, so I tossed the box under the bed and hid behind the door until she passed so I could walk right out the way I came in. I knocked on the front door not thirty minutes later, saying I was there to meet the Master MacLeod at his request. It was then, with much *shock and regret,* we found the man *dead!*" His voice was filled with contempt. It took everything I had, but I tried to keep from showing any emotion.

"I wrote the letter to yer laird as we all *grieved* this tragic loss, from his own desk, with his own paper and ink. Did ye not see that I used the black seal from the Advocate Society on the letter?"

I did not acknowledge the ask. I had noticed the black wax seal was one I had not seen before, but realized now that it matched the seal on the back of the Advocate Society invitation. Still, I never knew about the society, so let it go. I swallowed deep only because I had to hear the rest of the story and he just exposed one more mystery we needed to solve.

"How did ye come to put the name of my husband—a man you didna ken—on the marriage contract?"

Will placed his hands again on my back to support me.

"I met yer *husband* at Dunmara Castle. He was clearly in love with ye," he said, navigating both his memories and his plentiful drink. "I kent ye were not betrothed, but when I found that the man accompanied ye to Edinburgh, I put his name on the contract I secured to cause ye pain—or at least to question all the men surrounding ye. *Did my plan work?*"

I said nothing to him of this awkward and half-hearted ploy and moved right along to ask, "And yer return *when I was* in the house on Canongate?"

With my words, I could feel Will come stand closer to me and his hand, already placed on my back, began rubbing his finger slowly for support. We all knew I was going to have to relive what this man did to me—to us. And it will hurt everyone in this room.

"Och, even *easier*," the disgusting man said, gulping from his glass. A glass I can only thank Auld Jonah for constantly filling. Perhaps the freedom of drink is allowing us to hear the truth.

"I watched the house from the kirkyard fer many days and saw yer husband and stable master leave together. I kent ye were left with nothing but a wee mute lad scrubbing the front walk, an open close, and the auld missus in the courtyard tending her garden. Continuing what yer father started, ye arrived in Edinburgh and tried to take everything from me, and I was going to take it all from ye. I thought I had until I heard ye were still alive."

"What do ye care if I am alive? Have ye not set about yer own vengeance with the murder of Master MacLeod, the rape of his daughter, and the murder of her unborn child... *when will it be enough?*"

He did not answer me but gave me a cold stare and half-smile raised the hairs on the back of my neck. I already knew the answer to my own question. Calder believes the MacLeod's have ruined his life and deserve their fate. It would have been enough if *I were also dead.* Somehow, part of me wanted him to say the words himself. I needed Auld Jonah and everyone standing upright in this tavern to hear his confession and his intention for being here. Even though he knows that he is outnumbered, he seems determined to spend his last moments in this life hurting me and my family as much as he can. So, he finally said exactly what I hoped he would.

"I didna ken about a bairn, but if yer alive, *lass*, then my vengeance is not complete."

He knew about my bairn because I told him on that stone floor in the only moment of clarity I had after the fall. I pleaded for mercy that I was with child. He has decided to ignore that fact. I looked at Will and Duncan as I expected either of them to take a strike at the man on these words. In fact, I can now feel Duncan's hand on my back. He is silently asking me again to let him finish this. I could feel their anger and that they were tempted, but luckily, no man stepped forward against my orders. I could feel my own breath quicken.

I sat quietly for a moment and thought of one more question to complete the mystery of Allan Calder. I did not want to ask him about the torture of sending me the message and the gold watch chain in the village. I did not care anymore for his thinking on how to make me suffer or live in fear. I knew why he was here. He made it clear to all of us.

"Ye have been living rough fer some time. Surely a gold watch and a set of fine Scottish pearls could have been sold to give ye lodging, food, and drink. Ye could have even tried to go elsewhere and make a new life for yerself. Why are ye *here on Skye*, Calder?"

He just raised his shoulders and looked at me only to confirm what he said before, he was motivated by revenge on our family and nothing more. His possessions were mere trinkets designed to entice me back to him for his final acts of torture. And they worked. Here I sit before this horrible man!

"Ye cannae think that coming here would end well fer ye," I said. He remained quiet. He was on his mission of torment and nothing else. He could not complete his revenge the way he wanted, so he would hurt me with the truth of his confessions. That was enough for me. It was enough for all of us.

I breathed in deep and said to my knights as I stood up "Tie the man up and put him on the back of a horse."

I left the man in the company of men who could kill him in an instant, and he knew it. He tried to fight them for a moment, but he had no chance to take the three tall MacLeod clansmen towering over him and filled with rage.

"Yer dogs, once again at yer command, lass!" He yelled to me as I ignored him and his continued dismissal with the use of the term *lass*.

I grabbed Will's hand and said as I looked in his eyes, "Ensure he has no weapons on his body and bring me the watch and the pearls."

"Aye, my lady."

I stopped at the bar top as I put on my cloak and said to Auld Jonah, "I assume ye heard this man's confession, sir?"

"Aye, Lady MacLeod, and my heart breaks fer ye. It does," Jonah said as he bowed his head in reverence.

I left him more than enough coin he needed for our night in his tavern, our filled glasses, and for keeping Calder here for us. "Ye may be asked to account fer what ye heard one day.

"I ken, and I will, m'lady!"

I gave him a weak smile in appreciation and left the tavern as my knights tied Calder up and put him over the back of Will's horse that he would walk back toward Castle Dunmara.

Will brought me the watch and pearls and said nothing. He just kissed me softly on my cheek. I looked at father's watch and saw the names, *Flora, Alexandra, James'* engraved on the back, and I smiled at the thought of him carrying us, his family, with him every day. I kissed it and put the recovered items in my bodice of my dress, against my own heart.

Once we left the tavern and passed the stone markers showing we were well within MacLeod clan lands, I stopped Munro and the travelers behind me. I got down on my own, giving my beloved instructions to wait for me in his ear. He nodded to me and nudged my shoulder before nuzzling my cheek. This beloved horse was another knight of the realm and gave me his full support. He has always been another knight of the realm and I loved him so for his allegiance.

"Take him down," I said, pointing to Will and Duncan. The men did as I asked without question. Angus took the reins of the horses so that Will and Duncan could stand on both sides of Calder and hold him by his arms in front of me. They were the biggest and the strongest, but they were also the closest to me and felt every ounce of pain we felt as a family for what this man did to my father and then to me.

I saw my Munro dip his head to me once more as he subtly reminded me of my own strength and the honor and responsibility of my position. Strength that I have been summoning since Edinburgh, even in unhealthy ways. A strength I still have. Today, I represent my father and my clan, and *this man* cannot take that power and honor away from me with his cruel acts of vengeance.

I stood before Allan Calder and waited for him to look me in the eye. Once he did, I said calmly with my head held high, "As the chief of Clan MacLeod, one of my primary responsibilities is to ensure that my kinsmen are safe and protected. I will *always raise a shield* against anyone that comes fer my family or any member of this clan. It is my responsibility and duty."

Everyone went deathly silent.

"At this moment, sir, ye are standing in the heart of the MacLeod clan lands—our beautiful, majestic, and *peaceful* lands."

I held my arms wide in acknowledgement of the beautiful green lands of home surrounding us all. I could hear the water from the pools nearby and I could smell the sea that was waiting for us just over the next hill. These *are* beautiful lands. No one said a word. I waited until I could say what I needed to without emotion.

"Allan Calder, ye *confessed* to the trespassing—twice—on property, not yer own. Ye *confessed* to the murder of my father, Alexander Ewan MacLeod, and to the theft of his personal property that we recovered from ye this day. Ye *confessed* to the rape and beating of his only daughter, an act that resulted in the death of an unborn child—a bairn that would have been Alexander MacLeod's first grandchild."

Calder just looked at me without emotion. I saw both Will and Duncan lower their heads upon my words, though I could not bear to look at either of them. I said nothing of the inner hurt and turmoil he inflicted on our entire family since the death of my father and the lasting suffering and fear the man has caused me personally. His vengeful torture will be shown forever on the scars on my arm and my thigh and within my own mind. I kept Laird Graham's voice in my head, telling me that my tears were my own and this man only needed to be aware of his own pain at this moment. So I swallowed every single tear I had.

Calder's knees buckled slightly while he was still held by the arms of the strong men standing next to him. He knew this was his fate from the beginning. He had to know that coming here to stand before us all and making his confession that he would not survive this trip. The reality of such a decision seemed to be sinking in finally as his drink faded. For the first time now, he seemed fearful and his face a ghostly white—even more so than before.

"It is my responsibility to deliver justice on our clan lands. Sir, I find yer acts so *vengeful* against this clan and of this *family*, that I cannae in good conscience allow such a *threat* to remain here," I said as brought my sgian-dubh from my skirt and slid it under his ribs. His eyes remained on mine, though they fluttered for a moment in his pain. He opened his mouth, but he never made a sound.

No one balked for a moment or tried to stop me. Though I am certain my husband wondered how and when I retrieved my own blade. I dared not look at anyone but Calder. I twisted the knife and raised it even further into his chest as I said in his ear, *"That is my judgment this day as Lady MacLeod of MacLeod."*

The man's knees buckled. I pulled the blade out and calmly wiped it on his shoulder before putting it back in its sheath and mounting Munro for home. Duncan and Will finally let the man fall fully onto the ground.

When I got back on my horse, Duncan asked again with a slight smile, "What would ye would like us to do fer ye, my lady?"

This time, I finally answered my uncle's question with a cold and definitive order as Lady MacLeod. "Dispose of his body and please, for my sake and the sake of our family and clan, ensure he is truly dead when ye do. I can see the man is still breathing."

"It is time for us to go home, my Munro," I said softly into the ears of my gallant horse.

+++

Will joined me at Cairn's Point, where I had finally released all the tears I swallowed after hearing such a vile confession. I sobbed into his shoulder as he held me tight.

"Och, my love, ye were so strong and brave today! Ye got the truth of it. It was nothin' but vengeance on ye and yer father. *Nothin' but vengeance!*"

"I wanted to kill him, Will," I said as the tears flowed. I handed the sgian-dubh back to him with a shaky hand that still had Calder's blood on it.

"Keep it, love," he said, pushing it back to me. I earned my right to have a blade on my person again. I am certain he hoped that I would not hurt myself with the ghost of Allan Calder no longer haunting me. I hoped the same.

"Tell me what happened after I left ye."

"Ye were right. Calder was still alive. He was gravely wounded, but alive. We could have waited for him to die on yer cut, but instead Duncan gave me and Angus a moment to each take out our own rage on the man."

I could see now that Will's right hand looked much like it did after he beat Wesley MacLeod in the stables. I brought his hand to my lips and kissed his bruised knuckles in appreciation for his defense of his wife and family. I could not imagine what it took for him to hold back today and what he released at that moment of final retribution.

"Duncan ended him by crushing his skull with a rock, and I think he was most satisfied finishing what he started at the tavern."

"Where is Calder now?"

"Look just there," Will said, pointing over my shoulder to a small boat in the water before us. It was a mere speck in the dying light of the setting sun, but I could see it.

"Angus told us that the back part of Castle Rock has a lower shelf than the front. I rode ahead and secured a boat fer them at the south beach so they didna have to ride onto the castle grounds with the man's body on the back of a horse. They will strip Calder naked and put his body out to rot at the mercy of the birds and the weather."

I watched Angus and Duncan row the boat out against the waves, determined to complete their mission together. I had my own satisfaction at the thought that Calder could no longer hurt us as I put my hands to my face and cried as William held me tight. We watched the men in the boat eventually make their destination and then begin their return, this time with the waves supporting them on the return home.

"Our verra own *Prometheus of the rock*," I finally said under my breath to Will when I could speak again.

"*Prometheus?*"

"Greek mythology," I said, further lifting the veil of fear I had carried for so long.

"What?"

"Prometheus was a god of fire and he angered Zeus by giving fire to man. As punishment, he was bound to a rock so that every day, an eagle—representing his laird—would eat his liver only to have it grow again overnight so that he could be tortured again the following day in the same manner."

"*Christ above!*" Will said, looking back out at the rock.

"We will watch the birds for days to come, knowing Calder cannae hurt us anymore, in the never-ending torment of his own body—even if he is gone from this world."

"Aye, my love. Now it is Calder's blood and bones that can seep into the crevices of the stone. Fitting justice, I think," he said, remembering what I said about lying on the flagstone floor at Canongate.

I nodded in agreement and said invoking Master Shakespeare and *Macbeth* as I hugged him tight, *"What is done cannae be undone."*

Will looked at me with a smile upon my Shakespearean reference and kissed me gently. He said softly, *"Aye, my lady. It cannae. And I believe ye have yer own Prometheus."*

"Fitting justice, I think."

+++

After completing their mission, Angus and Duncan joined us at Cairn's Point. Duncan, covered in the man's blood and his own sweat from their rowing against the sea, came straight for me and hugged me tight. He almost picked me up off the ground. Neither of us wanted to let go of the other.

"It is over, lass! Erm, my lady! *It is over!*"

We were crushed by what we heard today, but in some ways also relieved to know the truth of it and to end the haunting specter of Allan Calder, Esquire. Duncan knew better than anyone what I felt and how I have struggled. For the first time, I realized that part of my own haunting had to do with the unfinished confirmation of how my father died suddenly after his return to Edinburgh. I think I always knew, but could not find the words. I could not prove my suspicion. But the mysterious missing wood box and the reappearance of the watch and pearls told me something was amiss.

"Aye," I said, wiping his tears with my very own handkerchief pulled from my skirts.

"Since when do ye have yer own handkerchief, lass?" he asked, laughing through his own tears.

"My husband used part of his dowry to buy me some of my very own," I said, repeating his instruction to Will before Master Forbes when the dowry was read.

"Verra fine! Verra fine, indeed!"

We stood silently for a bit before he put his hand on my shoulder and said, "My lady, my darling lass, I never thought I could be prouder of ye. Ye got the truth of Calder's vengeance, sittin' before the horrible man with a patience and a strength I wish I had myself. I am verra sorry I broke yer command when the man said what he did about Alexander."

"No sir," I said, kissing his cheek and hugging him tight, "I honestly dinna ken how ye beat us all to the punch!"

Duncan nodded on this and said after a moment, "My darlin' I dinnae ken how Will and I did not kill the man on what he said about ye. Ye ken I will regret leaving ye alone fer the rest of my life!"

Will and Angus hung their heads in the same shame Duncan felt. I know that he meant the words, but it was not completely fair.

"We are all to blame, including me, fer what happened. And we all have to let our regrets and shame go with the death of the man!"

He smiled at me, and I smiled back at him in understanding. I had one more thing to say.

I walked to Angus and kissed him on his cheek and hugged him tight across his shoulders. I am not sure I have ever hugged Angus before. The man seemed shocked at this show of such overt and genuine affection. He seemed wary at first, until he finally melted in my arms and hugged me back. This battlefield warrior is at his core, a very sweet man, a beloved cousin, and a trusted knight of Clan MacLeod. He lifted me from the ground and spun me around. We all started laughing and relishing the same relief and joy.

"My dear cousin, deep down, I always kent yer frequent trips to the Old Stone would benefit yer clan one day!"

Duncan laughed loudly and said, "Angus has been of the same mind fer years!"

Angus laughed before he nodded to me with respect. I smiled at him and said earnestly and with tears in my eyes for another man I love, "I thank ye, sir. Truly."

Angus smiled and stood tall as he said in a voice, we could all understand, and that of an honorable and dutiful soldier, "It has been my 'onor, m'lady."

Duncan said, "Alex, in Edinburgh, ye asked us to stay within the letter of the law and ensure that man got his well-deserved justice. Well, *yer the law* on MacLeod lands. I believe with everything that I have, that as hard as it was for ye, *yer justice* was the way this nightmare was supposed to end."

These men could not fully understand what I carried with me or battled inside my head since the intruder left MacLeod House on Canongate, and I could not speak to their own pain. We all have scars—

some are just more visible than others. We have carried each other's pain along with our own because we love each other.

Will spoke and said in a proud agreement of Duncan's words, "Ye did what ye had to for yer family and yer clan, and ye did it well, my lady."

I stood between them and took Will's hand and then Duncan's as we looked out at Castle Rock as the first birds began circling, much to the satisfaction of the audience standing on this cliff.

Will softly aid in my ear, *"Yer our lady, but yer now finally the Queen of Castle Rock."* I looked up at him and smiled at his words and remembrance of our conversation the night before we left for Edinburgh together.

Perhaps this was also what Master Garrick tried to tell me about *making a choice*. I could not imagine being here with anyone else than these beloved and wonderful men. All four of us made our own choice for our future. That choice was to be free of the ghost of the intruder, the pain of Edinburgh, and to love and support each other—as a family. I stood proud and confident because of the three men I had standing next to me on this promontory.

I always saw my shield as a defense against others...and it is. But my protective shield was never just my own. Only when I let these incredible men in did I realize the strength I had on my own was magnified by the strength and love that surrounds me.

A new sense of peace and strength came over me as I welcomed their protection and released every one of the old wounds and ghosts that I had been carrying all this time. *Finally, I released them all!*

Some went back into the cairn behind me.

Some were sent into the crashing waves below.

And some were given willingly to the hungry birds circling the skies above Castle Rock.

+++

GRATITUDE

Completing one novel seemed like a feat, but to have prepared a series was both unexpected and thrilling. I am proud to continue Alexandra's story.

I returned to Scotland in August 2022. I stayed again for a month to complete the edits on the second and third books of the *HOLD FAST Series*. I would like to thank everyone I met along the way who made my story even better or just lifted my spirits as I worked.

That starts with my friends **Cameron and Ross at SCOTCH at The Balmoral Hotel, Edinburgh**. Cameron shared the book, *Scotch Missed: Scotland's Lost Distillerie*s by Brian Townsend. Thinking about early distillery formation in the late Eighteenth Century, I took some liberties and let Alexandra be exactly like her father... *ahead of her time*. The broader distribution of whisky and thoughts of marketing the name Glenammon are early for the country during this time. But I will let this remarkable young woman lead exactly as her father did. The lessons I learned will only help my next book in the series. It will focus on the reclamation of Glenammon and the growth of the brewery and distillery operations on Skye in future books.

I would also like to acknowledge **Giovanni**, bar manager at **Bar Prince at The Balmoral Hotel, Edinburgh.** He and his incredible team always make me feel welcome and never balk at me sitting at the end of the bar with my laptop. I have always felt at home at this hotel, but it was truly my friends at the bar that encouraged and supported my progress on the completion of four novels this year. I thank them all!

Once again, I must acknowledge the **National Library of Scotland** for being a constant source of insight and information and a welcome refuge when I am in Edinburgh. I am proud of my library card (though my photo is not the best!) and have loved my time in the reading rooms. Each manuscript, book, or file I reserved over the last fourteen months influenced my writing and my own understanding of the country and time. The extensive archives and real examples of 18th century wedding contracts, wills, clan land documents, and even recipes, made my books in this entire series richer. The sheer amount of documentation was overwhelming, but such an honor and privilege to see first-hand.

I would like to thank **my colleague and friend Angela Curran.** As a fellow author, Angela encouraged me to not only find the outlet of creative writing outside the corporate walls of Microsoft but gave me the first suggestions on how to get started self-publishing, how to manage my own expectations, and provided many resources to keep me going throughout my journey as I continue to learn. Angela's words—and that of the Seattle writer's group she invited me to join in the early stages of development—provided encouragement that rang in my ears from the beginning to the end of this endeavor, and I owe her a sincere debt of gratitude.

I would also like to thank many of **my friends and former co-workers Christina Watt, Nicole Christie, and Deirdre Quarnstrom** that I let in on my *writing project.* All of them encouraged me to stay focused on my own personal writing outside of work in some way and made me feel in every interaction that I should keep doing what made me happy. Additional support included writer's workshops I should consider, general feedback on the earliest drafts, or even sharing the published books with others beyond my own network. I am so glad I listened to all of them. I have never been happier in my life!

I continue to have gratitude for the talented **Jared Frank** (@visualether on Instagram). His incredible cover art and design made each of my books come to life and made my promotion ability easy. I love his collaborative sprit and his creative work. He embraced Alexandra's story from the start and brought my series to life in more ways than I could ever imagine. Each cover perfectly captures the spirit of Scotland and each stage of Alexandra's story. Seeing the first three books together makes me so proud! They naturally and beautifully fit together.

Every visit to Scotland reminds me I am *home*. On each of my trips, I crossed all parts of Scotland with a cheering section wishing me well, willingly connecting me with others, and helping me in any and every way they could. Many of my edits and additions were from these incredible people and places on my journey—not just academic research.

I am looking forward to my next trip during Christmas and Hogmanay in 2022/2023. I hope to promote and market the series more, being on the ground in the country that inspires me. I will also continue my research for my upcoming novels.

ABOUT THE AUTHOR

 Cynthia Harris is the author of *HOLD FAST*, her debut novel and the first novel of the historical fiction *HOLD FAST Series*. With *RAISE YOUR SHIELD*, she delivers the third installment in the series. She is also the author of her first contemporary romance novel, *Fun & Games*. All of her novels are available in paperback and Kindle versions on Amazon.com.

Cynthia built a career in storytelling. From leading advertising and marketing strategy for some of the world's most recognized consumer brands, international news organizations, and major league sports teams—to leading internal and external communication strategy and speech writing for technology, human resources, gaming, and entertainment executives—words have not only been her passion, but her livelihood. With her novels, Cynthia now focuses her time on finding and sharing her own voice.

As a proud graduate of The University of Georgia, she made a home in the Pacific Northwest over sixteen years ago. She keeps her gas tank full and her passport current, so she can escape to the incredible places near and far that allow her to revisit history, fuel her creativity, and find peace. But Scotland is calling, and she is currently looking for a new home in the country that she loves.

FROM THE AUTHOR

Thank you for reading! But don't worry! I fully expect to continue the *HOLD FAST Series* in the coming year. Like many of you, I have also fallen in love with Alexandra, William, Duncan, and Angus. I want you to follow the rest of Alexandra's story and her growth as Lady MacLeod, and I believe that the men who love her have their own stories to tell.

If you liked *RAISE YOUR SHIELD*, Book 3 of the *HOLD FAST Series* (or even if you didn't), I'd appreciate a quick review on Amazon, so I know how to make my books better and what you want to read from me in the future. Your feedback also helps other readers discover my work.

If you want to preview some of my writing, get sneak peeks of future work, or learn about my journey as an author, visit me at cynthiaharrisauthor.com or follow me on Instagram at cynthia_harris_author.

Cynthia Harris Novels

Fun & Games

HOLD FAST
Book 1 Of The HOLD FAST Series

A STRENGTH SUMMONED
Book 2 Of The HOLD FAST Series

RAISE YOUR SHIELD

Book 3 Of The HOLD FAST Series